She expected him to kiss her, was ready for it.

But nothing in their previous contact had prepared her for the electric jolt when he took her lower lip between his teeth. The slow, erotic nips generated shiver after shiver.

Jill gave fleeting thought to her mission, to the need to maintain distance. And then her conscious mind shut down. As greedy now as he was, Jill arched her spine to increase the contact. At that, Cody dragged his mouth from hers and forced himself to speak.

"If we're going to stop this celebration," he ground out, "we'd better do it now."

He was giving her the choice. Jill blew out a ragged breath. "I vote we continue the celebration and see where it takes us."

"Oh, I can tell you right now where it'll take us," he warned. "The question is, are you sure you want to go there?"

Dear Reader,

This year may be winding down, but the excitement's as high as ever here at Silhouette Intimate Moments. National bestselling author Merline Lovelace starts the month off with a bang with *A Question of Intent,* the first of a wonderful new miniseries called TO PROTECT AND DEFEND. Look for the next book, *Full Throttle,* in Silhouette Desire in January 2004.

Because you've told us you like miniseries, we've got three more for you this month. Marie Ferrarella continues her family-based CAVANAUGH JUSTICE miniseries with *Crime and Passion.* Then we have two military options: *Strategic Engagement* features another of Catherine Mann's WINGMEN WARRIORS, while Ingrid Weaver shows she can *Aim for the Heart* with her newest EAGLE SQUADRON tale. We've got a couple of superb stand-alone novels for you, too: *Midnight Run,* in which a wrongly accused cop has only one option— the heroine!—to save his freedom, by reader favorite Linda Castillo, and Laura Gale's deeply moving debut, *The Tie That Binds,* about a reunited couple's fight to save their daughter's life.

Enjoy them all—and we'll see you again next month, for six more of the best and most exciting romances around.

Yours,

Leslie J. Wainger
Executive Editor

Please address questions and book requests to:
Silhouette Reader Service
U.S.: 3010 Walden Ave., P.O. Box 1325, Buffalo, NY 14269
Canadian: P.O. Box 609, Fort Erie, Ont. L2A 5X3

MERLINE LOVELACE
A QUESTION OF INTENT

Silhouette®

INTIMATE MOMENTS™

Published by Silhouette Books

America's Publisher of Contemporary Romance

SILHOUETTE BOOKS

ISBN 0-373-27325-8

A QUESTION OF INTENT

Copyright © 2003 by Merline Lovelace

Books by Merline Lovelace

MERLINE LOVELACE

spent twenty-three years in the U.S. Air Force, pulling tours in Vietnam, at the Pentagon and at bases all over the world. When she hung up her uniform, she decided to try her hand at writing. She's since had more than forty-five novels published, with over seven million copies of her work in print. She and her own handsome hero live in Oklahoma. They enjoy traveling and chasing little white balls around the fairways.

To Tammie and Dr. Dave—
thanks for all the years of fun family holidays
and the expert medical input for this book!

Chapter 1

"Rattler One, this is Rattler Control."

U.S. Army Major Jill Bradshaw took her gaze from the moon-washed desert landscape and smiled as she keyed the transmit button on her handheld communicator. When her small detachment of military police had first gathered at this supersecret test site, she'd left the choice of a call sign designator to them. After hot debate, they'd settled on Rattler in deference to the deadly diamondbacks nesting under just about every rock and bush in this patch of southeastern New Mexico. The call sign was also intended to symbolize the fact that her tough-as-nails military cops intended to inject pure poison into anyone who attempted to penetrate their remote site.

"This is Rattler One," Jill replied. "Go ahead, Control."

"The sensors are indicating a breach of the perimeter."

"Is the intruder of the two- or four-legged variety?"

"I make it four-wheeled."

After two weeks of installing the active and passive defenses for the hundred-square-mile site that ranged from flat, dry desert to high, pine-studded mountains, every member of Jill's team had become adept at differentiating between the varying signals emitted by the sensors. They could ID a jackrabbit on the run and the coyote chasing him, as well as the occasional hunter who missed—or ignored—the Restricted Area signs and strayed onto the site.

"The vehicle was moving at approximately forty miles per hour but is now stopped."

Stopped? Jill didn't like the sound of that. "Give me the coordinates."

"Alpha-three-zero-eight, kilo-six-one-two."

She thumbed the digits into the number pad of her eBook. The handy-dandy, palm-held device was only one of the new pieces of equipment being tested in conjunction with the supersecret Pegasus Project. The small apparatus acted as a document viewer and terminal to receive data and graphics. When teamed with a body-worn computer, it gave soldiers the ability to perform computational operations, store data, view maps, coordinate troop movements, and communicate quickly and directly with one another. At thirty-one, Jill considered herself a fairly savvy representative of the electronic generation, but the whiz-bang capabilities of this palm-size gizmo continued to astound her.

"I make the intruder only a few miles from my present location," she told the controller.

"That's how we make him, too."

"I'll check him out. Contact the patrol in sector five and have them stand by in case I need backup."

"Roger, One."

Jill thumbed a button to activate the directional finder of the eBook and hooked the device to the dash of her souped-up dune buggy. Standard patrol cars didn't hack it out here in the desert, where there was a whole lot more sand than tarmac. Her detachment drove a fleet of highly maneuverable ATVs fitted with mountings for a small arsenal of weapons and the latest in high-tech navigational aids. The distinctive Military Police markings on the side of the vehicle left no doubt as to who manned them.

Despite the markings, Jill and her security forces had orders to keep as low a profile as possible in conducting their duties. Most of the intruders her troops had intercepted in the past two weeks had left the area convinced they'd stumbled onto a remote patch of the Army's White Sands Missile Test Range. Even the residents of Chorro, the sleepy, one-gas-station town some thirty miles west of the site, didn't know an entire test complex had been shipped in and assembled in less than two weeks.

Looking back, Jill could only marvel at all that had been accomplished in those hectic two weeks. Working around the clock, her people had completed a security grid of the entire test site and set up the perimeter defenses. Prefab buildings had been trucked in, assembled, and were ready for occupancy. Racks and racks of highly sophisticated test equipment had been uncrated and set up. U.S. Navy Captain Sam Westerhall, the tough, grizzled leader of the joint service project had hit the site yesterday. The rest of his multiservice test team would arrive tomorrow.

The day after, Pegasus would roll or fly or swim in—Jill wasn't quite sure which. She, like the other key members of the test cadre, would find out more about the top-secret project at the team's in-briefing tomorrow.

Tonight, though, she had another fifty or so miles of perimeter to run, two patrols to check on and an intruder to intercept. She eyed the directional finder on the eBook, saw she was still two miles to target, and pressed down on the accelerator.

The wizard in charge of her fleet had modified the ATV's mufflers to all but kill its normal growl. As Jill jounced along the narrow, two-lane dirt road, the quiet of the vast Chihuahuan Desert surrounded her.

The seemingly endless patch of sand was primarily scrub and shrub. The ubiquitous creosote bush with its tarry scent and perforated branches popped up everywhere, interspersed with yucca, saltbush, and a small, night-blooming cactus that blinked delicate white eyes in the vehicle's headlights.

Although naturally partial to her native Oregon, Jill had to admit the Chihuahuan Desert was pure magic at night. The wide-open spaces merged earth and sky until she couldn't tell where one stopped and the other began. She felt as though she was aiming her vehicle straight at the bright, glittering stars that seemed to dangle directly in front of her.

She didn't consider herself a romantic by any means. Few of the cops she'd worked with over the years would think of themselves that way, she suspected. Yet that incredible, sparkling curtain made her wish she had something of the poet or artist in her soul.

Tearing her gaze from the spectacular view, she checked the directional finder again. A mile to target. Slowing, she killed the headlights and activated the night-vision navigational system. A screen built into the dash showed the road ahead in glowing green detail. Night navigation would make for slower going, but there was no need to advertise her approach to the intruder if he hadn't already spotted the spear of her vehicle's headlights.

He could be anyone, she reminded herself as she

navigated only by the light of the moon and the directional finder. A lost traveler, confused by the long, empty stretch of dirt road that cut through the desert. A hunter out to get a jumpstart on a dawn shoot. A Mescalero Apache from the reservation to the north, following in the footsteps of the ancestors who'd roamed over this land at will.

Or someone not quite as innocent.

A smuggler trucking in illegal aliens. A noisy reporter who'd gotten wind of the sudden influx of people into the area. Or a terrorist, out to sabotage the top-secret weapon the United States government hoped would be the instrument of his destruction.

Jill might not know the specifics of Pegasus Project, but the general who'd called her in and told her she'd been hand selected to head the security detail at the test site had stressed it would be a prime target for attack if word leaked out what was being done here. She'd been allowed to pick every man and woman on her detachment and had chosen only the best of the best. To a person, they were fully prepared to lay down their lives if necessary to defend the site from physical, biological or chemical attack.

"Let's hope it doesn't come to that," she muttered to the plastic, bobble-headed Goofy stuck to her ATV's dash with Velcro.

She wasn't superstitious. Not at all. But good ol' Goof had gone through four years of ROTC with her at the University of Oregon, had sweated through the grueling Military Police Officers' basic and advance courses at Fort Leonard Wood, Missouri, and accompanied her on assignments all over the globe, including Kosovo and Iraq. If she ever found a man with his long, gangly build and stupid grin, she would probably jump his bones on the spot.

Of course, the fact that Goof was the direct physical opposite of the smooth, slick, rock-you-back-on-your-heels-handsome bastard she'd tangled with her freshman year at OU might have something to do with her preference for the anatomically challenged. Shoving the memory of that grim event back into the black hole where it belonged, she checked the directional finder again, slowed the ATV to a halt and keyed her communicator.

"Control, this is Rattler One."

"Go ahead, One."

"Unless the target has moved, I'm within fifty meters of his position."

"He hasn't tripped any more sensors. We make him at the same coordinates we gave you earlier."

"Roger, Control. I'm leaving my vehicle to recon on foot."

"We'll track you, One."

Jill checked her equipment before leaving the vehicle. She carried five spare clips for her pistol on her webbed utility belt, along with a set of handcuffs, a nightstick and the long, heavy flashlight that could come in real handy if she didn't have time to reach for her nightstick. She stuffed additional clips for her semiautomatic rifle in a side pocket on the belt and flicked a finger to set Goofy bobbing.

"Watch my six, fella."

He nodded his vigorous concurrence. That was another thing she liked about ol' Goof. He never disagreed with her.

Clipping the communications device to her breast pocket, Jill tucked an errant strand of her blunt-cut blond hair under her black beret. Although the Rangers and Special Forces had raised howls of outrage when the Army brass decided to issue berets to all soldiers, she had to admit the headgear looked a lot meaner than the standard BDU patrol cap.

BDU. Battle Dress Uniform. What idiot had coined that term? There wasn't anything dressy about the baggy, green-brown-and-black camouflage pants or the matching shirt worn with sleeves rolled up to form a constricting band just above the elbow.

Swinging out of the ATV, Jill slung her rifle over one shoulder. The case containing her night-vision goggles went over the other. Fully armed, she started for the target. The August night was hot and dry, but not uncomfortable…except on her feet. The desert sand had absorbed the fierce August sun all day and was now giving it up. The heat came right through the soles of her boots.

Toasty-toed, she topped a small rise and stopped to take a reading. Affirming she was aimed in the right direction, she pulled out her night-vision goggles and squinted through the viewers. The endless vista spread out before her took on a greenish glow, brighter in some spots than others because of the heat still rising from the sands.

And from the still-warm engine of the SUV directly ahead of her.

The vehicle was parked beside a clump of jagged rock that thrust up out of the desert floor. It was one of those big, muscled monsters, favored by ranchers and yuppies alike. A Chevy Tahoe or Ford Expedition, judging by its extended frame. Jill scanned it from bumper to bumper, but saw no sign of the driver. Silently she moved close enough to make the license tag.

"Rattler Control," she called in softly. "This is Rattler One."

"This is Rattler Control. Go ahead, One."

"I have the vehicle in view. Run a twenty-eight/twenty-nine on New York tag Lima-Echo-Alpha-six-four-four."

"Will do, One."

Jill waited while the controller put the license number through the National Crime Information Center. He was back with the requested information in less than a minute.

"The tag checks to a corporation called Ditech, Limited. The vehicle is listed as a 2001 Lincoln Navigator and doesn't come back stolen."

"Roger, control." She swept the area again, searching the open stretches of desert and the shadowed rocks some distance from the parked SUV. "I don't see the driver. I'm going in to check out the vehicle."

Her boots crunching on the sand, she approached the midnight-blue Lincoln and aimed her flashlight at the darkened windows. The powerful beam confirmed there was no one sitting behind or slumped over the wheel. A cautious circuit of the vehicle showed all four bucket seats were empty. A roll-out shield covered the rear luggage compartment, giving no clue as to its contents.

Frowning, Jill made another circuit, aiming the flashlight at the ground this time. The sand was hard here, not like the snowy, fine-grained white stuff farther north, but her boot prints showed clearly enough. As did the faint indentations leading toward the rocky outcropping.

Jill eyed the single set of prints. Their size and shape suggested a male. A big one. That didn't particularly worry her. She'd learned enough tricks over the years to take down any two drunken soldiers stupid enough to get crosswise of her. What worried her was why the heck this guy had stopped just inside the perimeter of the Pegasus site.

Easing her semiautomatic rifle from her shoulder, she nestled it in the crook of her arm and rested her finger on the trigger guard. The M-9 was light enough to carry easily for long distances and accurate enough to be fired on the run. Jill could attest to both attributes from past experience. Aiming the flashlight at the tracks, she followed them toward the rocks.

"There's a set of footprints in the sand," she advised Control, tilting her chin down to speak softly into the mike. "I'm following them to... Damn!"

What happened next was just the kind of unexpected situation she'd learned to anticipate in her years as a cop. Still, she just about jumped out of her boots when a shadowy figure suddenly rounded the rocky outcropping and almost collided with her.

"What the hell!"

His deep snarl shattered the stillness of the night. Jill danced back, her heart pumping pure adrenaline, and whipped up both her weapon and the flashlight. She caught a glimpse, only a glimpse of his startled expression before he, too, reacted with razor-edged instincts. One moment he was squinting into the blinding light. The next he was hurtling through the air like a NFL linebacker with a ten-thousand-dollar bonus riding on his next quarterback sack.

Jill's instincts were every bit as quick. She danced to the side and resisted the impulse to bring the butt of her rifle down on the man's neck as he barreled past. She'd been trained to use force only as a last resort, but she wasn't above stacking the odds in her favor by thrusting out a boot.

He went down with a grunt and a thud that raised

puffs of sand. If she'd been out to cuff him, she would have barked out an order for him to plant his face in the dirt at that point. Instead, she stood well away from his feet and kept a wary eye on his hands as he rolled onto his hip. As an added precaution, she aimed the powerful flashlight right at his face, effectively blinding him.

He threw up an arm to shield his eyes from the intense light, allowing Jill to catalogue his wavy black hair, a square jaw and powerful shoulders under an open-necked red knit shirt. The rest of his body matched the shoulders, she noted in a swift sweep. Narrow waist, lean hips, well muscled thighs that strained the fabric of his well-washed jeans. She also made note of the gold watch circling his left wrist.

The Lincoln and the obviously expensive watch suggested he wasn't a hunter or a smuggler running illegal aliens. Nor did he look like your average lost tourist. A few years ago Jill might have said he didn't look like your average terrorist, either, but the Oklahoma City bombing proved even clean-cut, ex-Marines were capable of committing the most despicable acts of violence.

"Is that your vehicle parked by the road?" she asked, keeping him pinned in the flashlight's beam.

"Yes."

"Who are you and what are you doing in this area?"

"The name's Richardson. Cody Richardson."

Jill sucked in a quick breath. She recognized the name, if not the face. Commander Cody Richardson, Public Health Service. Dr. Richardson, if she accorded him his title instead of his rank.

Jill had thoroughly reviewed the background dossiers and security clearances of every test cadre member, including that of Dr. Richardson. But the head-and-shoulders photo of the PHS officer assigned to the Pegasus Project didn't come close to matching this hunk of raw maleness. The subject of that photo had worn wire-rim glasses, a white lab coat and scowled into the camera as if annoyed at being disturbed.

This man wore a red knit Polo shirt that clung to his wide shoulders and a pair of worn jeans that displayed lean hips and muscled thighs. Evidently the doc—if he *was* the physician and brilliant researcher expected at the site—believed in keeping himself in shape.

Squinting at her from under his upraised arm, he rapped out a question of his own. "Who are you?"

"I'm Major Jill Bradshaw, United States Army."

Some of the belligerence seeped out of him. "U.S. Army?"

"That's right."

His tense, corded muscles relaxed. "Sorry I came at you the way I did, Major. Chalk it up to the fact that you surprised the hell out of me. I saw the rifle pointed straight at my middle and my self-preservation instincts kicked in.''

When she made no comment, he angled his head behind the shield of his upraised arm, trying to see her.

''How about you get that light out of my eyes.''

''How about you show me some ID?''

The cool response didn't win her any Brownie points with the doc. Above the muscular forearm, his black brows snapped together. ''My wallet's in my back pocket.''

''Get up, plant your hands against the rock, and spread your legs. Please,'' she tacked on after a moment.

He rolled to his feet with an athletic grace that didn't impress her a bit. The butt-head who'd attacked her in college had been a star skier, golfer and swimmer. Personally, Jill preferred the gangly, gawky type.

She patted him down for hidden weapons, then asked him to extract his wallet from his rear pocket. Slowly. Carefully. He did so, turning around to hand her the slim leather billfold. She examined both his driver's license and Public Health Service ID card. The ID confirmed he was, in fact, the expert in biological agents who'd been tagged to work the Pegasus Project, but Jill still had a few questions that needed answering.

''May I ask where you were headed?''

"I'm en route from San Antonio to San Francisco. I decided to cut across country and pick up I-40 in Albuquerque, but took the wrong road out of El Paso."

She gave him full marks for a good cover story. He must have figured out by now she was with the Pegasus security team but wasn't going to admit it until she asked for the code. She took her time doing so.

"Why did you stop here? Did you run out of gas?"

"No."

Neither his expression nor his stance altered, but Jill didn't miss the slight hesitation before he continued.

"I stopped to admire the view from the top of the rocks," he said ruefully, as if admitting to an embarrassing character flaw. "It's pretty awesome."

Yeah, right.

Jill had been a cop too long to accept a trite explanation like that. Particularly when it was accompanied by a grin that showed a flash of even white teeth and crinkled the skin at the corners of too-blue eyes. If Dr. Cody Richardson had left his vehicle to climb the rocks, her instincts told her it wasn't to admire the view.

Still, Richardson had been cleared for this project by the highest levels at the Pentagon. He matched the physical description in his dossier, more or less.

He wasn't supposed to arrive until tomorrow but could have made good time on the road and decided to press on. Jill saw no other choice but to put him through one more gate.

"Do you have the time, Dr. Richardson?"

He bent his elbow. She caught another flash of gold and the ripple of muscle under his knit shirt when his shoulders lifted in a shrug.

"Sorry, my watch seems to have stopped."

Jill dipped her head to acknowledge that he'd given the proper response. Something about this guy still didn't sit right with her, but he'd passed every test. Filing away the nagging little doubt for further examination later, she handed him back his wallet and rendered the salute he was due because of his superior rank.

"Welcome to Site Thirty-Two, Dr. Richardson."

He returned the salute with a precision that surprised her. Although the Public Health Service was one of the seven uniformed services, the members of their small officer corps were more noted for their medical expertise than their strict adherence to military customs and courtesies.

"My vehicle's just over that rise," she informed him. "Wait here until I retrieve it, then I'll escort you to the compound."

Cody slipped his billfold into his back pocket and watched the major stride off into the darkness.

Damned if the woman hadn't taken five years off his life, popping up out of the desert the way she had.

Given the security briefings he'd received after being selected for the Pegasus Project, Cody had fully expected to be challenged when he arrived at the test site. He just hadn't expected that challenge to take place out here, in the middle of nowhere. Or in the form of a bristly female soldier.

Well, maybe not all that bristly. The woman's smooth sweep of silky blond hair softened the Amazon image considerably. Not to mention the trim, tight butt he'd taken note of when she turned and strode off. Despite the beret, combat boots and bulky web belt with all its accouterments, Major Jill Bradshaw looked pretty good in her BDUs. Cody ought to know. He'd studied the human form in all its variations for going on fifteen years now.

Lord! Was it really that long since med school? That many years since he'd tumbled into love with a bright-eyed Red Cross volunteer? Those days at Duke seemed as if they'd happened in another life. To a different man.

They had, he thought grimly as he yanked at the Navigator's door. An entirely different man. Or so Alicia had claimed the night she'd stormed out of their house three years ago. Her last, furious tirade haunted Cody to this day. Not even a velvet night and a brilliant tapestry of stars could ease his soul-searing guilt.

He wasn't about to admit he'd stopped out here in the middle of nowhere in the vain hope of finding solace, though. Particularly to a tough, no-nonsense military cop.

Wrapping his hands around the steering wheel, he stared into the darkness and waited for the major's vehicle to appear.

Chapter 2

Radioing ahead, Jill advised Navy Captain Sam Westfall that one of his key team leaders had appeared on the scene well ahead of his estimated time of arrival.

"I'm escorting Dr. Richardson to the compound now."

"Good," the commanding officer replied in his deep, gravelly bass. "Bring him to my quarters when you arrive."

"Will do, sir."

Hands on the ATV's wheel, Jill navigated the dirt road shooting straight as an arrow across the desert. The headlights of Doc Richardson's SUV speared through the darkness behind her.

"I don't know about this guy," she muttered to Goofy as she flicked a glance in the ATV's rearview mirror. "He sure doesn't look like any brilliant research scientist I ever stumbled across."

Not that she'd stumbled across all that many. After the brutal assault in her freshman year and a subsequent bungled investigation by the campus police, Jill had made up her mind nothing like that would ever happen to her again. She'd switched her major to law enforcement and enrolled in every available self-defense course available off-campus. And once she'd been commissioned as a military police officer, she'd pretty well lived, breathed, eaten, and slept in her fatigues. She hardly knew *anyone* who wasn't a cop, much less a brilliant scientist.

"Think I'll take another look at his dossier," she murmured to Goof. "Something about his roadside stop to drink in the stars just doesn't sit right with me."

Mickey's pal bobbed his head in vigorous agreement, as he always did.

Some forty minutes later, Jill slowed for the first checkpoint. The MP who came out of the modular booth that served as a guard shack recognized her in the glare of the spot angled down from the shack's roof. The sergeant saluted respectfully but still asked for ID. Jill handed him a flat leather case, pleased that he hadn't let her pass on mere visual recognition.

He aimed a small electronic sensor at her face,

then ran it over her holographic ID. The flat, credit card size bit of plastic contained an astonishing array of photo imaging, retinal scan data, fingerprints, DNA information, and a special code signifying Jill's level of access within the compound. The card also contained a built-in signal transmitter that allowed the Control Center to track the movements of the person carrying it. When the card reader gave two soft pings, the sergeant handed her back the leather case.

"You're cleared for entry, Major."

"Thanks. I'm escorting Dr. Cody Richardson to the site," she told him, pointing a thumb at the vehicle behind hers. "He's on your key personnel list."

"Yes, ma'am."

The sergeant walked back to the idling SUV and requested the doc's civilian ID. Angling his flashlight at Richardson, he scrutinized the physician's face and compared it to the photo before taking the identification back into the guard post to check the access list. Tomorrow Jill would issue each of the cadre members a holographic ID similar to hers and considerably speed up the entry process.

After some moments the guard returned to Richardson's vehicle and handed him back his ID. "Do you have a camera, computer, cell phone, or other electronic device in your vehicle, sir?"

"Just a cell phone."

"Sorry, sir. I'll have to take that."

"Right."

Reporting instructions had advised all cadre members not to bring their own computers or electronic notebooks. Encrypted versions would be issued to them. The same instructions had advised that personal cell phones used en route would have to be turned in on arrival. Any calls coming in to those phones would be routed through the Control Center to secure instruments on-site.

Once cleared, the doc followed Jill's vehicle down another lonely five-mile stretch of road. The compound lights were mere pinpricks in the distance, almost indistinguishable from the bright wash of stars. Gradually, the pinpricks grew brighter and closer.

Jill stopped at a second checkpoint, this one guarding a cluster of prefabricated modular buildings and trailers surrounded by rolls of concertina wire. In the wash of lights mounted at regular intervals within the compound, the main site had all the charm and warmth of a lunar moonscape. There wasn't a tree or a bush to be seen. White-painted rocks marked the roads and walkways between the buildings. Off in the distance, the hangar that would house Pegasus loomed over the rest of the structures like a big, brooding mammoth. Aside from a few picnic tables scattered among the trailers, everything was starkly functional.

Guards at the second checkpoint cleared Jill through. She waited once more for the doc, then drove across the compound to the trailer housing the commanding officer of the Pegasus test cadre. The Lincoln's tires crunched on the hard-packed dirt as it pulled up beside her ATV. Cody Richardson climbed out, thudding the vehicle's door shut, and gave her a questioning glance.

"These are Captain Westfall's quarters," Jill informed him. "He requested I bring you here."

Nodding, Richardson followed her to the trailer. Jill's knock brought Westfall to the door. The tall, spare Naval officer was still in his working khakis, which didn't surprise her. The captain had only arrived on-site yesterday morning, but Jill had already formed the distinct impression he wasn't the type to retire early or sleep late.

"This is Dr. Richardson, sir."

She stepped aside, allowing the Public Health Service officer to brush by her and offer a crisp salute.

"Sorry I'm out of uniform, sir. I didn't expect to report to you tonight."

"Not a problem, Doc. Come in, come in." Westfall speared Jill with one of his penetrating, steel-gray glances. "Thanks for delivering him, Major. Everything quiet out on the test range?"

"It is now."

The captain raised a brow. Before Jill could elaborate, Richardson offered a cool explanation.

"The major and I ran into each other. Literally. I ate sand until she decided I was who I said I was."

"Did you?" He tipped Jill an approving nod. "I'll see you tomorrow at the in-brief."

"Yes, sir."

After an exchange of salutes, she made her way to her vehicle. Instead of driving back out to run the perimeter and check her patrols, however, she headed for the squat, dun-colored modular unit that served as her detachment's headquarters and operations center.

A welcome blast of chilled air greeted her when she stepped inside, along with the even more welcome scent of fresh-brewed coffee. Rattler Control occupied the rear half of the unit; her cubbyhole of an office, the armory, and a small break area took up the front half.

She stopped at the armory first to turn in her rifle and ammo clips. That done, she made a beeline for the coffee. Filling a jet-black mug emblazoned with her unit's self-designed crest—a rattlesnake coiled around the crossed Revolutionary-War-era pistols designating the MP Corps—she stuck her head inside the control center.

"I'll be in my office for a while."

"Yes, ma'am." The lanky Oklahoman at the dispatch console spun his chair around. "That was some takedown out there."

"Nothing like putting one of our own facedown in the dirt," Jill agreed.

Specialist First Class Denton grinned. "I'm guessing that Public Health weenie will think twice before taking you on again.''

''I wouldn't exactly classify Dr. Richardson as a weenie,'' she replied, remembering the breadth of the man's shoulders.

''Whatever he is, he's the first to get a taste of Rattler venom. Good goin', Major.''

Jill bowed to the inevitable. She knew the story of her brief confrontation with Cody Richardson was going to be repeated—and greatly exaggerated—by every one of her troops. Which wasn't necessarily all that bad. She was long past the point of having to prove herself to either her people or to herself, but a little Marshal-Matt-Dillon-style action never hurt a cop's image.

''I'll be in my office,'' she repeated, retreating while her invincible aura still glowed bright and strong.

Once in her closet-size cubbyhole, she wedged behind her desk and placed her mug on the red blotter. A quick click of the keyboard activated her computer. The sleek laptop was state-of-the-art, its hard drive encrypted and shielded against penetration by everyone from Kremlin spies to everyday, average teenage hackers.

The screen hummed to life and blinked open to a screensaver featuring an Army tank in full attack mode. Jill entered her access code, pulled down the menu marked Personnel and zeroed in on Dr. Cody

Richardson. Mere seconds later his file painted across
the screen. A click on the thumbnail sketch of his
picture enlarged it to screen size.

There he was, glasses, white lab coat and all. With
the same annoyed expression he'd worn earlier this
evening. And the same square chin, which she'd
somehow overlooked before. The guy was a Clark
Kent, she decided, seemingly innocuous looking in
his everyday work disguise. Very different out of it
and in the flesh.

Irritated with herself for forming a preconceived
concept based on a sterile looking lab environment
and a white coat, she opened the doc's background
file. His credentials had impressed her the first two
times she'd read them. They still impressed her.

"Graduate of the University of North Carolina,"
she muttered under her breath, "with honors in
chemistry and biology. M.D. from Duke. Completed
an internship and residency in internal medicine, with
a follow-on fellowship in clinical pharmacology and
infectious diseases at Johns Hopkins. Masters in Public Health from Harvard."

Scrolling down the screen, she skimmed over
Richardson's professional associations, publications
and work history. He'd spent several years practicing
medicine before going to work for a major pharmaceutical company. If Jill was reading all this technical stuff correctly, he'd then moved into the forefront
of the battle against AIDs and Ebola. Three years

ago, he'd jettisoned his job with the pharmaceutical giant to join the Public Health Service.

Jill didn't know all that much about the PHS, except that it was a corps of approximately six thousand uniformed officers within the Department of Health and Human Services. These highly trained health professionals operated within all divisions of HHS, including the Center for Disease Control, the National Institute of Health and the Food and Drug Administration. They also served as a mobile force to provide primary health care to medically underserved rural and Native American populations. Cody Richardson had joined their ranks three years ago.

"Bet you took one hell of a pay cut when you made that move," Jill murmured.

If so, he was still living off the proceeds of his former life. Lincoln Navigators and flashy gold Rolexes didn't come cheap. She made a mental note to check into the corporation the Lincoln was registered to and continued scrolling through his file.

Heading a team of researchers at the National Institute of Health, Richardson had helped isolate the West Nile virus. He also, Jill saw, worked closely with the military services to test and field countertoxins to various biological agents. Because of that work, he'd been hand selected to test the nuclear, biological and chemical defenses installed in Pegasus. In addition, he and a small staff would provide on-site medical care for the test cadre.

Richardson's personal data was considerably more concise. Parents alive and living in North Carolina. No siblings. Wife deceased. No children.

Leaning back in her chair, Jill took a long swig of her coffee. Dr. Richardson's file painted a portrait of a dedicated, hardworking physician who was also a brilliant research scientist. Nothing in what she'd read suggested a predilection for stargazing.

She'd keep an eye on the doc, she decided. A close eye. Shutting down the screen, she finished her coffee and went back to the Control Center to check the status of her deployed patrols. Just after 1:00 a.m., she called it a night.

"We have a big day tomorrow," she reminded her dispatchers. "The rest of the test cadre is scheduled to arrive between 8:00 a.m. and noon."

"We're ready for 'em," SFC Denton advised in his Oklahoma drawl. "Our welcome committee will have 'em roped, tied and branded a half hour after they hit the site."

"Tell the welcome committee to start with Dr. Richardson. I want him tagged first thing in the morning."

"Yes, ma'am."

Jill woke before dawn the next morning. She stretched catlike under the sheet and enjoyed the quiet of the boxy modular unit that served as her quarters. She'd had the three-bedroom, one bathroom unit to herself for the past couple of weeks. After today she'd share it with two other female officers.

Her mouth curved in a wry grimace. She wasn't much for girl talk or gabfests. She hoped the other women weren't, either. Probably not. One was a Coast Guard officer with several command assignments under her belt. The other a hurricane hunter with the National Oceanographic and Atmospheric Agency.

Thinking of all she had to do to get ready for the onslaught of arrivals, Jill threw back the sheet and padded to the bathroom. After a thorough scrub of face and teeth, she dragged a brush through her straight, blunt-cut bob. The straw-colored strands fell neatly into place thanks to a great cut, just brushing her jawline but well above the top of her uniform collar as required by Army regulations. A slather of lotion to protect her face from the dry New Mexico heat and a quick swipe of lip gloss completed her morning beauty regimen.

Jill had long ago found ways to satisfy her feminine side other than through cosmetics that didn't mix well with camouflage face paint. Her neatly trimmed nails wore a coat of French-white polish, and her underwear tended more toward lace than spandex. No one could see her frilly undies under her BDUs and T-shirt, so she figured her tough-cop image was safe.

She chose an ice-blue set this morning. The bikini

pants were cut low on her belly and high on her thigh. The lacy bra contained no underwiring. She didn't carry a particularly generous set of curves on her trim frame and saw no need to torture herself with hard-wired cups. Ten minutes after slithering into the slinky underwear, she was booted, bloused, belted and ready for the day.

Six hours later, her uniform had wilted a little in the searing hundred-plus-degree heat, but all eighty-two of the Pegasus cadre members were safely on-site. Helicopters had ferried most of them down from Albuquerque, where they'd flown into either the civilian airport or the Air Force base on the city's outskirts. A number had driven in, including one of Jill's new roommates.

Lieutenant Commander Kate Hargrave had thoroughly impressed the gate guards by showing up at the checkpoint in a low-slung, ground-eating XJS. She impressed them even more when she climbed out of the Jag, revealing a pair of long, tanned legs and the lush curves of a *Playboy* centerfold.

With her troops' break room right outside her office, Jill couldn't help but overhear their vivid descriptions of the sexy hurricane hunter. A chance meeting with the woman outside the dining facility where the cadre was gathering for the in-brief proved her troops hadn't exaggerated.

"Major Bradshaw?"

At the sound of her name, Jill turned to see the tall, leggy redhead weaving her way through the crowd. Since her Navy-style rank of lieutenant commander was the equivalent of Jill's Army rank of major, the two women shook hands instead of saluting.

"I'm Kate Hargrave. I understand we're going to be sharing a bathroom for the next few months."

Hargrave's crisp, tailored khaki uniform in no way disguised her hourglass figure, but her cheerful smile drew the eye as much as her curves. Jill's eye, anyway. Most of the males going by kept their gazes well south of her nameplate.

"I haven't shared a bathroom with anyone since I dumped my jerk of an ex," the weather officer confessed with a grin. "I hope you don't spend as much time in there reading the newspaper as he did."

Jill couldn't help but respond to that infectious grin. "Not to worry. I doubt any of us will have time to read a newspaper in the next few months."

"Good. I like to keep busy. From the little I've been told about this project so far, we're all going to have our hands— Whoa!"

The woman's green eyes widened and fixed on something just over Jill's shoulder.

"Things just got interesting," she murmured in a low, throaty purr. "Very interesting."

Jill turned and saw at once what had snagged her attention. Dr. Cody Richardson was striding across the compound. Public Health Service Officers also wore Navy-style uniforms. Jill had to admit Dr. Richardson wore his khakis *extremely* well.

The man could have modeled for a recruiting poster. His pants were knife creased, his short-sleeved shirt tailored to maximize the effect of his muscled torso. Black shoulder boards carried the broad gold stripes denoting his rank. The insignia on his cap featured a caduceus crossed with a fouled anchor, denoting the Public Health Service's original charter to provide medical care to America's sailors. Beneath his cap, Richardson's eyes gleamed a killer blue against his tanned skin.

''Who *is* that?'' Kate Hargrave breathed.

''Commander Cody Richardson,'' Jill answered. ''Public Health Service.''

''That's the doc who's going to be taking care of our every little cough and stubbed toe? Well, well.''

''I believe his primary duty will be to test the nuclear, biological and chemical defenses installed in Pegasus.''

Jill had no idea why the response came out sounding so stiff. It wasn't any skin off her nose if Kate Hargrave wanted to fall all over the man.

As he approached, both women acknowledged his senior rank with a salute. Richardson returned it, gave the redhead a smile, and addressed Jill.

''Good morning, Major.''

She dipped her chin in a polite nod. "Good morning."

"Sleep well after our little tussle last night?"

From a corner of her eye, she saw her new roommate arch an auburn-tinted brow. Jill kept both her voice and her smile even.

"As a matter of fact, I did." With a nod at her companion, she performed the introductions. "Have you met Lieutenant Commander Kate Hargrave? Or do you prefer Dr. Hargrave?" she asked the weather officer, mindful of the string of initials after her name.

"In uniform, I use my rank." Smiling, she offered the doc her hand. "But among friends and cohorts, it's Kate."

"Kate," he acknowledged, taking her hand in his. "I spent most of last night reviewing medical records. Yours were particularly interesting."

Jill just bet they were.

"I'd like to hear more about your reaction to the vaccine you were administered after exposure to the Nipah virus in Honduras last year. Your records indicated you went into shock."

Well, that was one of the more original pick-up lines Jill had ever heard. Evidently Kate thought so, too. She flashed Richardson a hundred-megawatt smile.

"Anytime, Doc."

When he blinked, looking more than a little

stunned, Jill checked her watch and suggested they continue their conversation inside.

Excitement hummed through the air inside the large, open dining area. Jill and the other two joined the group of officers at the front of the room. A petite brunette introduced herself as Lieutenant Caroline Dunn, Coast Guard. The buzz-cut marine beside her was Major Russ McIver. The senior Air Force rep arrived a moment later. Before he could make the rounds and introduce himself, a voice bellowed at the back of the crowd.

"Room! Ha-tennnn-*shun!*"

Eighty-two backs went blade stiff. One hundred and sixty-four knees locked. Chests out, arms straight at their sides, hands curled into fists, the entire test cadre stood at rigid attention while Captain Sam Westfall strode to the podium at the front of the room. Even the few civilians almost lost among the sea of uniforms squared their shoulders.

The captain kept the group at attention while his gray eyes skimmed the room. There wasn't a sound. Not so much as the shuffle of a foot or the creak of a sagging floorboard. When it seemed he'd looked every man and women present in the eye at least once, Captain Westfall put them at ease and told them to take their seats. When the scrape of chairs and rumble of everyone getting settled had died, he gave the room at large a flinty smile.

"I think you should know up-front I've reviewed

the personnel files on each and every one of you. Most of you I handpicked for this assignment. You represent the best of the best from each of your services, all seven of which are represented in this test cadre. For that reason, you'll be issued a special unit patch during in-processing.''

With a nod, he signaled his executive officer to come forward. The Army captain carried a large poster, placed it on a metal easel, and flipped up the top sheet. Underneath was a classic shield-shaped design. The bottom two thirds of the shield was red. The top third showed a blue field studded with silver stars.

''Please note we've included one star for each of the seven uniformed services,'' Westfall pointed out, reaching into his shirt pocket for a collapsible pointer. He extended the metal rod and issued a request. ''I'd like the senior representative to stand as I name their service. In order of precedence, they are…''

The pointer's tip whipped against a star.

''The United States Army. Founded June, 1775.''

As the senior Army officer on-site, Jill stood and acknowledged the chorus of hoo-ah's that rose from the grunts in the audience. When the noise faded, the captain's pointer whapped another star.

''The United States Navy, founded October, 1775. I have the honor of being the senior rep from the sea service.''

The squids responded with a stamp of booted feet.

"The United States Marine Corps, founded November, also 1775."

Major Russ McIver, the senior leatherneck present, led a round of "Semper Fi's."

"The United States Coast Guard, dating back to the Colonial Lighthouse Service established in 1789 and the Revenue Cutter Service, founded shortly thereafter."

Lieutenant Caroline Dunn stood. The only Coast Guard rep assigned to the test cadre, the petite brunette rendered a smart salute.

"Next," Westfall continued, "the United States Public Health Service, which traces its origins to the 1798 act that provided for the care of America's sick and injured merchant seamen."

"That's me," Dr. Richardson said, standing to nod at the crowd.

"The National Oceanographic and Atmospheric Agency, established in 1870."

Kate Hargrove was the NOAA rep to the cadre. When the gorgeous redhead stood to acknowledge her service, a murmur of masculine appreciation rippled through the crowd.

"Last but certainly not least," the captain said with a nod to the blue-suiters in the audience, "the United States Air Force. Formerly the Army Air Corps, it was established as a separate service in 1947."

The AF senior rep was a tall, ramrod-straight pilot with salt-and-pepper hair and laugh lines around his eyes. Belying his status as a member of the ''baby'' service, Lieutenant Colonel Bill Thompson looked tough and experienced and well able to serve as deputy director of the Pegasus Project.

Westfall let the assembled crowd enjoy the spirit of good-natured rivalry for a moment or two before continuing.

''Each of the seven uniformed services has a history rich in tradition. Each has provided long years of honorable service to our country. I know you're proud, as I am, to wear the distinctive insignia of your branch or corps. I would remind you, though, of the oath each of you took when you joined the military. To protect and defend the Constitution of the United States. That oath transcends your individual services. As of this moment, your first allegiance will be to each other…and to the project that has brought us here.''

At a nod from the captain, his exec added an overlay to the shield. When the transparent overlay settled, a milky-white winged stallion reared on the field of red, white, and blue. Westfall let everyone in the room get a good look.

''Welcome to Project Pegasus, ladies and gentlemen. We are now one team, with one mission. Before any of us leaves this corner of the desert, the new all-weather, all-terrain attack/transport vehicle known as Pegasus will be certified to run with the wind, swim the oceans and fly to the stars. Your country is depending on you to make it happen.''

The terse pronouncement killed any tendencies toward levity among the assembled personnel.

''You'll receive more detailed briefings on the vehicle when it arrives tomorrow. Today you'll get security and area threat briefings, be issued your site IDs and go through a medical screening.''

The captain collapsed his pointer with a snap.

''Major Bradshaw, I'll turn the group over to you now.''

''Yes, sir.''

Jill stood at attention with the others while Captain Westfall departed. When he'd cleared the building, she moved to the podium. As she looked out over the sea of faces, the realization that she was responsible for both their safety and their adherence to ultrastrict security measures hit her smack in the chest.

One compromise of classified test information, and her neck would be on the block. One physical breach of the Pegasus site, and she could kiss her career goodbye.

Her glance slid to Cody Richardson, lingered a moment, shifted back to the crowd at large.

''Good afternoon, ladies and gentlemen. I'm Major Jill Bradshaw. My security forces and I are going to be watching out for you—and watching over you—for the next few months.''

Chapter 3

Cody hooked his stethoscope around his neck and scribbled an entry in the form on the clipboard. Sixty-five patients in three and a half hours. Seventeen more to go.

All that was really required today was an intake exam—temperature, blood pressure, heart rate, updated health history, etc. The small team of highly skilled corpsmen assigned to the Pegasus site could have handled those tasks easily. Cody had wanted to meet each of the test cadre members personally, however, and get their take on their physical, emotional and mental condition.

If the first sixty-five were to be believed, he thought wryly, Captain Westfall had assembled the healthiest military team in the history of the universe. Only one had a condition that required watching. Lieutenant Colonel Bill Thompson, the Air Force rep, had mild atrial fibrillation, the most common form of heart arrhythmia. It was a lifelong condition that didn't require medication or he wouldn't have been cleared to fly. As a result, Cody didn't anticipate having to spend a whole lot of time here in the clinic. Good thing, since providing medical care to the folks on-site was only the secondary reason for his presence out here in the middle of the desert.

Thinking of the twists and turns his life had taken to bring him to this place and this time, he tipped his chair against the wall. Slowly, inevitably, the familiar poison of guilt and regret seeped through his veins.

How the hell had things gone so wrong? Why hadn't he seen the train barreling along the tracks before it ran right over him? How had he managed to lose himself long before he lost Alicia?

Knowing he'd find no answers to the questions that had plagued him more than three years now, he shoved his chair back and rejoined his team in the clinic area.

"Who's next?"

"Major Jill Bradshaw," a white-suited corpsman replied, handing him another clipboard. "She's in cubicle two."

A ripple of completely unprofessional anticipation

feathered along Cody's nerves. He'd been waiting for this particular patient.

"Is Petty Officer Ingalls with her?"

"Yes, sir."

Hospital Corpsman Second Class Beverly Ingalls was one of only two women on Cody's medical staff. She'd assisted him in the exam of other females assigned to the Pegasus cadre. She'd assist him in this one, as well.

As he walked toward the curtained cubicle, Cody skimmed Jill Bradshaw's chart. Her vitals looked good. Better than good. So did her physical stats. Age, thirty-one. Height, five-seven. Weight, 121. Nonsmoker. Occasional social drinker. No history of serious or debilitating diseases.

Lifting the curtain, he nodded to the woman seated on the exam table, swinging a boot impatiently. "Hello again, Major."

"Sir."

She ran a quick glance down the white coat he wore over his uniform and cocked her head. "No glasses?"

"I beg your pardon?"

"The photo in your background file shows you in a lab coat and wire-rimmed glasses. I sort of assumed the two went together."

"Not anymore. It got to be a pain sliding my glasses up on my forehead whenever I bent to look in a microscope so I had Lasik surgery earlier this

year.'' He flipped through the forms on the clipboard.
''I skimmed through your medical history. On paper
you look pretty healthy.''

In Cody's considered opinion, she looked pretty
darned good in the flesh, too. Her skin glowed with
a rosy tint that owed more to exercise and a sensible
diet than cosmetics, and her corn-silk hair had a
smooth, glossy sheen that dared a man to run his
hands through it. Resisting the impulse, he handed
Petty Officer Ingalls the chart and dragged his stethoscope from around his neck.

''Unbutton your shirt, please.''

While the major slipped the buttons on her BDU
shirt, Cody wrapped himself in a cloak of professional detachment. Or tried to. For reasons he didn't
stop and analyze at the moment, he had trouble view-
ing Major Jill Bradshaw with his usual impassive
objectivity.

If any of the patients he screened in the past ninety
minutes was going to rouse the male in him, Cody
would have bet money on the flame-haired knockout.
Lieutenant Commander Hargrave filled out a uniform
like no one he'd ever examined before. Yet he'd experienced no more than a fleeting appreciation at her
perfect symmetry of face and form. In contrast, he
felt his breath hitch as Jill Bradshaw's hair parted to
give him a glimpse of soft, white nape.

Suddenly Cody stiffened. Beneath that spun-gold
silk lay one of the most vicious scars he'd seen since

his E.R. rotation at Raleigh's busy Memorial Hospital. The puckered seam of flesh tracked a path from just behind her left ear to her collar before disappearing under the crewneck of her regulation brown T-shirt.

"Someone left you quite a souvenir," Cody commented, reaching up to finger the ridged flesh.

She jerked away as if stung. A quick rake of her fingers through her hair settled the sleek cap over the scar. The reaction intrigued him as much as the wound.

"Did you get that injury in the line of duty?"

"No."

The curt reply suggested the subject was off-limits. Cody ignored the warning. "Knife or broken glass?"

"Neither."

She flicked him an annoyed glance, saw he wasn't going to go away, and shrugged.

"The cut was made by the jagged edge of an aluminum beer can. The jock I was out with had been demonstrating his intellectual prowess by ripping them in half with his teeth. I tripped, fell on one, and walked away with a permanent reminder of the consequences of consorting with idiots."

"You're lucky you walked away at all. Another inch to the right and you would have severed your carotid artery."

"So I've been told."

There was more to the story than that, but the glint

in her brown eyes said that was all Cody would get. Today, anyway. He'd find out the rest of the tale sometime in the very near future, he promised himself as he plugged in the eartips of his stethoscope.

Jill left the clinic more rattled than she wanted to admit. What *was* it about the man that set off her silent alarms? It wasn't just her usual conditioned response to big, too-handsome types. Or her still-unanswered questions about why he'd stopped to contemplate the night sky. This guy got to her in a way no man had in longer than she wanted to remember.

She'd had to force herself not to react when he'd leaned over her to press the stethoscope amplifier to her back. She'd also done her damnedest to ignore his unique blend of aftershave and antiseptic, but the scent seemed to follow her when she walked out into the slowly purpling dusk.

After two weeks she was still getting acclimated to New Mexico's spectacular sunsets. With reds and pinks and blues pinwheeling across the sky, she reviewed her plans for the evening. She'd hit the northeast sector, she decided. Run the perimeter where it cut across the southern tip of the Guadalupe Mountains.

First, though, she would chow down. The fluttery feeling in her stomach probably had nothing to do with the doc and everything to do with the fact she'd gobbled a honey-oat bar and three cups of coffee for breakfast and been too busy for lunch.

The scent of sizzling steak drew her to the dining facility. With the arrival of two additional cooks, the kitchen was now in full operational mode. After two weeks of prepackaged meals supplemented by their one cook's valiant attempts to set up the kitchen and serve at least one hot entree, Jill was ready for a full-course dinner.

As during the earlier in-brief, the dining facility buzzed with the lively conversation of people getting to know one another. A quick glance told Jill members of the individual services had pretty much clumped together. Natural, she supposed for the first night. Once the test project swung into full gear, the service lines would break down and they'd meld into a team. Hopefully!

To aid the process she opted not to join her military cops and took her tray to a table of Air Force blue-suiters instead. In quick order she met a range instrumentation technician, a vehicle maintenance specialist and a computer systems analyst. The motor pool sergeant talked the universal language of transmissions and drive shafts, but the instrumentation expert and the analyst soon lost Jill in the technical dust. She left the dining facility knowing at least three of the test cadre a little better.

When she returned to her quarters just after 10:00 p.m., she got to know her roommates, as well.

Kate Hargrave had obviously just returned from a run or a workout in the site's small gym. A sweatband held back her sweat-dampened hair. Tight biker shorts clung to her trim thighs, and her gray jersey top sported damp patches. She'd abandoned a pair of well-used running shoes and was busy applying a coat of cherry-colored polish to her toenails.

Caroline Dunn lounged in the one comfortable chair in the unit, a paperback novel propped in front of her nose. Like Kate, the brunette had changed out of her uniform and wore a stretchy lycra halter with elastic-waist shorts. Lowering the book, she sent the newcomer a warm smile.

"There you are. Kate and I were about to give up on you."

Jill barely suppressed a groan. After running a long stretch of perimeter and checking on two patrols, sand had seeped into every pore. All she wanted was to hit the shower and the sack.

"We didn't get a chance to talk much at the in-brief," the Coast Guard officer said, laying her book across her bare midriff. "Since we'll be sharing a head and a living space smaller than the ward room on my first patrol boat, I thought it might make the next couple of months easier if we confessed to any weird habits or personal preferences right up-front."

Not a bad idea, Jill thought, giving the coastie full marks. With all her years aboard ship, Dunn had probably raised the art of sharing cramped quarters to its highest level.

"Sounds good to me," she said. "Just let me shed my gear and grab something cold to drink."

"I brought in a few emergency supplies," Kate Hargrave put in, waving the polish brush toward the half-size refrigerator in the galley. "We have soft drinks, instant iced tea, a rather nice chilled Riesling, and beer."

A nice chilled Riesling, huh? Maybe this roommate business wouldn't be such a pain, after all.

Retreating to her bedroom, Jill shed her beret and heavy web belt. Ingrained habit had her extracting the .9mm Beretta from its holster and checking to see the safety was on before ejecting its magazine. A quick tug on the slide confirmed no round was chambered. Returning the weapon to its holster, she stripped off her boots and BDUs.

She was twenty pounds lighter and a good deal cooler when she returned to the living area in gray sweat shorts and an oversize red T-shirt with a grinning Goofy on the front. Placing her eBook on the counter that served as both desk and dining table, she poured some wine into a blue plastic cup and plopped down on one of the counter stools.

"Since this was my idea," Lieutenant Dunn said with a lazy stretch, "I'll start. I prefer Cari to Caroline and will warn you right up-front I'm addicted to gory police procedurals and international thrillers.

Reach for one of my Tom Clancy's or Robert Ludlum's before I've finished it and you'll lose an arm.''

If that was the worst of her roommates' idiosyncrasies, Jill figured they'd all make it through the next few months in one piece. She took a sip of her wine, savoring its light, fruity bouquet, while Cari turned the floor over to the next in line.

''Kate? How about you?''

''I'm easy.'' The weather scientist decorated another toe with a streak of cherry red. ''Nothing very much bothers me—with the distinct exception of poaching on another woman's territory. Comes from being cast in the classic cheated-on wife role.''

Cari winced. ''Ouch.''

''Yeah, ouch.'' Kate wiggled her foot to check out the paint job. ''Don't take me wrong. My husband and I didn't have what you'd call the perfect marriage. I had pretty much decided to break it off. What got to me was that I was too busy—and too stupid— to realize he'd already made the same decision. Only he'd made it in the bed of a nineteen-year-old bimbette. Now *that* hurt,'' she admitted with a wry chuckle.

''I'll bet.''

''Which is why I'm real careful to watch where I step. So what's with you and the doc, roomie? Do you two have something going?''

Jill sputtered into the plastic cup, sending a spray

of fruity bubbles up her nose. She sneezed them out and shot the other woman a quick frown.

"You're kidding, right?"

"Nope. I got the scoop on that tussle Cody mentioned. Sounds like the two of you had some fun out in the desert last night."

Cody, was it? Lieutenant Commander Hargrave didn't waste any time. It also sounded as though the rumor mill was already up and working. Nothing like a small, isolated site to bare every wart and wrinkle.

"Look," Jill said carefully, "I don't want to get off on the wrong foot here, but I don't think what happened between Dr. Richardson and me last night is—"

"Any of my business?" Kate finished with one of her flashing grins. "It might have been, if I hadn't seen the way the man looked at you this morning. I was the invisible sidekick standing next to this woman," she added for Cari's benefit.

Somehow Jill didn't think the flamboyant redhead could ever qualify for invisible status.

"I checked him out for you," Kate announced, giving her little toe a final dab before capping the polish bottle. "He lost his wife several years ago, and he's currently uninvolved, so you wouldn't be poaching. Although I understand there's a media consultant back in Virginia who'd like nothing more than to sink her claws into the man."

Cari looked amused. Jill was astounded. "You've

only been on-site a little over eight hours. How did you find all that out?''

''I asked him. Not directly, of course, but he gave me sufficient information for my purposes.''

''Good grief! You're in the wrong profession. You ought to be in counterintelligence.''

''When I get tired of being buffeted around the skies, I might consider it. So back to my original question, Bradshaw. What are your intentions regarding our hottie of a doc?''

She probed with such breezy cheerfulness that Jill couldn't take offense. ''Dr. Richardson and I met for the first time last night. I barely know the man.''

''Hmm. My considered opinion is the doc would like to change that situation. It's only an opinion, mind you, but...'' She let her voice trail off suggestively.

Enough was enough. Jill wasn't about to admit Cody Richardson already occupied too big a chunk of her thoughts. Deliberately she changed the subject.

''I doubt any of us is going to have time for playing the kind of games you're suggesting. I had a peek at the preliminary test schedule. The whole on-site cadre goes into 24/7 mode after Pegasus arrives tomorrow.''

As she'd anticipated, she snagged the others' instant attention. Whatever their personal idiosyncrasies, they were each top-notch professionals in their respective fields. Kate dropped her cherry-tipped feet to the floor and leaned forward, folding her arms across her knees. Cari tossed her paperback aside.

"After I was cleared for this project, I read every report on Pegasus I could get my hands on," the Coast Guard officer said. "The test vehicle took some severe hits going through the research and development phase."

Kate nodded. "Congress tried to cut the program at every major milestone. The fact that two of the three initial prototypes crashed and burned didn't help matters."

"From what I hear, the president and the joint chiefs of staff are pinning all their hopes on us." Cari's small, heart-shaped face took on a grim cast. "If we don't demonstrate that Pegasus can swim..."

"And fly," Kate put in.

"And climb," Jill said, thinking of the steep mountains in the northeastern corner of the test site.

"...the services will be out a state-of-the-art, all-weather, all-terrain attack/transport vehicle capable of hunting down and ferreting out terrorists wherever the bastards try to hide," Cari finished.

Silence invaded the small living area as the three women felt the weight of their individual responsibilities.

"Well," Kate said after a moment, "I think I'll hit the rack. I want a clear head for the briefing tomorrow."

Cari pushed out of her chair. "Me, too."

She started for her bedroom, paused and turned back to Jill. "You never got a chance to tell us your likes or dislikes. Anything Kate and I should be aware of?"

"Nothing other than a propensity to receive alerts from my Control Center at any hour of the night and day." Jill palmed the small communications device that acted as her link to her on-duty controllers. "If I get called out, I'll try not to disturb you."

The Coast Guard officer tipped her a grin. "Don't worry about us. I've learned to snatch catnaps aboard ships plowing through gale-force seas. Kate, I imagine, has had to curl up in the back end of a plane and ignore the drone of four turbo-prop engines for hours on end."

"More times than I can count," the hurricane hunter drawled. "Neither one of us will break a snore if you get paged in the middle of the night."

Jill hadn't planned on testing her roommates' ability to tune out disturbances that very night. Some hours later, however, her communicator pinged and dragged her from a deep, dreamless sleep. She jerked her head up, blinking away the cobwebs, and fumbled for her communicator.

"Major Bradshaw."

"This is Rattler Control, ma'am."

Jill raked a hand through her hair and squinted at the digital clock beside her bed. Two forty-five.

"Go ahead, Rattler control."

"We have a report of an S-80."

Oh, jeez! Snakebite.

If Jill were ever dumb enough to let herself get talked into a show like *Fear Factor,* all they'd have to do is wave a harmless little garter snake in her direction and she'd concede the game right then and there. Anything poisonous—like the diamondbacks that owned this corner of New Mexico—sent chills skittering down her arms. Gulping, she keyed her communicator.

"I copy, Control. Who took the hit?"

"Sergeant Greg Barnes. He and Sergeant Kinnear are out on patrol. They're requesting immediate assistance. Dr. Richardson has been notified. We have a chopper warming up now."

"Roger, Control. Advise the doc I'll meet him at the helo pad."

Chapter 4

Jill threw on her uniform and stamped her feet into her boots. Less than ten minutes after receiving the call from Rattler Control, she pounded up to the helo pad. A UH-1 Huey painted in desert camouflage colors was shuddering and straining at the chocks. The chopper was older than she was—Vietnam-era vintage—but still the workhorse of the military.

Clamping a hand on her beret, she ducked under the whirling blades and darted to the side hatch. She got a boot on the skid and reached up to grab the flight engineer's hand. Mere seconds after she'd strapped herself in and pulled on a headset, the chopper lifted off. Sand blasted in through the open hatch until the nose rocked down and the pilot shifted from hover to forward motion.

Doc Richardson sat in the webbed seat beside her, his black bag clamped between his boots. He gave her a nod but said nothing until the lights of the compound had dropped out of sight and the pilot had locked onto a course that would take him to his patient.

At that point, he had the pilot patch him through to flight ops, who in turn patched him into the military police net. Both the doc and Jill listened intently as the control center raised the two-man patrol.

"Rattler Four, this is Rattler Control. Be advised medical assistance in the air and en route."

"Glad to hear that, Control."

Hear came out sounding more like he-ah. Jill smiled grimly at the Boston twang. If anyone would keep his head in an emergency, it would be Staff Sergeant Joe Kinnear, a bull-necked veteran with more than fifteen years as a military cop under his belt.

"The doc wants to talk to you," the Control Center advised. "I'm patching him through now. Go ahead, sir."

"Sergeant Kinnear, this is Dr. Richardson. Tell me the location of your partner's wound."

"Left calf, just above his boot top. Damned fangs went right through his BDUs."

"You didn't elevate the leg, did you?"

"Negative, sir. I've got him stretched across the seats in a neutral position."

"What's his condition?"

"Pretty calm, considering."

"What treatment have you initiated?"

"I let the wound bleed freely for a few seconds, cleansed it with Betadine from our snakebite kit and wrapped the Ace bandage around his calf just above the wound. I'm using the extractor pump as we speak."

"You're alternating the suction on the fang marks, right? First one, then the other."

"That's a rog, sir."

"Good man. How long have you been applying suction?"

"About fifteen minutes now."

"Are you seeing a white, milky substance mixed in with the body fluid as it comes out?"

"I did at first."

The terse reply had Jill clenching her fists.

"Now it's mostly just blood."

"That's a positive sign," Richardson said calmly. "You've probably drawn out all or most of the venom. Continue the suction until we get there. Be careful not to splash the extracted blood on yourself or the victim."

"Will do, Doc."

"We'll keep this channel open if you need to talk or ask any questions. Otherwise, I'll let you continue what you're doing."

Richardson's steady assurances soothed some of

Jill's jagged edges as well as those of the men on the ground. She uncurled her fists, splayed her hands on her knees and dragged in the first full breath since answering the call from Control Center. Pushing up the mouthpiece on her headset, she turned to the doc and pitched her voice over the *whap-whap-whap* of the rotor blades.

"Have you had a lot of experience with snakebite?"

"Some."

"Do you think Sergeant Barnes will be okay?"

"A lot depends on the type, age and size of the snake that bit him. But considering he hasn't gone into shock and his partner was so quick to apply an extractor to the wound, I'm hopeful."

Jill slumped back against the seat. Thank God she'd included new, commercial-brand snakebite kits in the list of mandatory equipment she'd submitted for her detachment. The kits cost a little more than the Army version, but their handy-dandy plastic extractor had already proven its value. She spent the rest of the short flight mentally reviewing the other survival equipment her troops had been provided.

To Jill's intense relief, Sergeant Barnes was a lot more blasé about his wound than she would have been. He greeted her and the doc with a grin when they dashed from the chopper to the ATV parked beside a moon-washed gully.

"Well, Major, looks like we got us a mascot."

Barnes nodded to a bundled BDU shirt that began to writhe and emit furious rattles at the sound of his voice.

"You trapped it?" Jill asked incredulously.

"Kinnear here did."

"The thing's fang caught in Barnes's pants," the sergeant explained. "It was either bundle it in my shirt and yank it off, or risk putting a bullet through Barnes's leg."

"How big is it?" the doc asked, planting his black bag on the floor of the ATV.

"Eight to ten feet of pure, hissing meanness."

Nodding, Richardson pulled out a pair of thin rubber gloves. The chopper's powerful searchlight added to the directed beams of the soldiers' flashlights and provided more than enough light for him to examine the wound.

"Looks good," he said when he'd removed the suction cup and gently probed the red, swollen flesh.

Barnes craned to have a look. Sergeant Kinnear's beefy hand planted him back down on the seat and kept him in place while Richardson dug into his bag.

"I'm going to remove the Ace bandage and administer an antivenin serum now. Given your size and the size of that rattler, I'll pump fifteen vials into you. That large a dose will make you whoozy, so don't get alarmed if your head starts to spin. Once the serum works its way into your bloodstream, we'll transport you to the chopper and back to base."

"Whatever you say, Doc."

Jill and Sergeant Kinnear stood back to give him room to work. The injections took only a few moments, but the wait for the serum to take effect seemed to stretch forever. Dr. Richardson reassured his patient by citing the high recovery statistics for snakebite victims, yet didn't minimize the possible side effects during the recovery process. He also voiced words of praise for Sergeant Kinnear's quick use of the snakebite kit.

"The major's the one who deserves the credit," the grizzled veteran countered. "She made sure we all received special training to counter venomous bites the first day we arrived on-site."

Richardson's gaze swung to Jill. "Smart thinking."

"Just doing my job."

She'd shrugged off the compliment, but the doc's warm approval pleased her more than she wanted to admit.

He voiced it again an hour later, after he'd turned Sergeant Barnes over to a corpsman to watch for the rest of the night.

"Kinnear's quick response may have saved his partner considerable discomfort and possible paralysis," he told Jill as he propped open the clinic door to allow her to precede him out into the night. "That, and the special training you provided your people."

"Working in this environment, it only made sense." She turned to face him, intending to call it a night. "Thanks for taking such good care of my troop."

His mouth curved. Solemnly he echoed her earlier response. "Just doing my job."

She'd already noted how the skin at the corners of his eyes crinkled when he smiled. Now she was forced to note the effect his smile had on her respiratory system. Frowning, she checked her watch. Four-thirty. Another forty-five minutes, and her alarm would start pinging.

"I'm too wired to go back to sleep," she said, surprising herself by adding a kicker. "Do you want to grab a cup of coffee?"

"Sounds good."

"My folks keep a pot on in our break area, but this time of night it generally runs to industrial-strength sludge."

"I can handle it."

She was beginning to believe he could. After observing him in action the past two nights, Jill had the feeling the doc could handle just about anything that came his way.

As she led the way to the squat modular unit housing the control center, she found herself reassessing her initial doubts about Cody Richardson. Maybe she was being too suspicious. Maybe he really had stopped beside the road to stargaze. And maybe she should find out more about the man than the dry facts she'd gleaned from his background dossier and the not-so-dry tidbits Kate Hargrave had supplied. That was the reason she gave herself, anyway, for suggesting they take their coffee to the picnic table outside.

"Just let me check in with my controllers and update them on Sergeant Barnes's status."

Cody listened absently to the murmur of voices in the other room as he dumped several packets of sugar and creamer into his coffee to dilute its tarlike consistency. The major left hers black, he saw when she returned. If she drank very much of this stuff, it was no wonder she stayed so wired.

Mug in hand, he followed her outside to a folding metal picnic table set a few yards from Control Center. The bench looked too narrow for comfort, so Cody opted to sit on the tabletop and prop his feet on the metal seat.

The major did the same. Dragging off her black beret, she jammed it in the pocket on her pants leg and made herself comfortable. A whisper of a breeze coming off the desert lifted the ends of her hair, washed to a silvery gold by the moonlight.

"My guys are already talking about constructing a pen for the rattler," she said with a grimace. "They want to make it our unit mascot. I agreed on the condition I never have to watch the thing being fed."

A companionable silence wrapped around them. Cody sipped his coffee, oddly reluctant to break it. Curiosity about the woman beside him finally prompted an idle question.

"How long have you been an MP?"

"Going on eleven years now."

"It's a tough profession."

"It can be."

"So tell me about it."

She slanted him a quick glance. "Why?"

He hooked a brow. "Oh, I don't know. Let's just chalk it up to a natural curiosity about women who plant me facedown in the dirt."

"That still rankles, does it?"

"Not particularly. But it does make me want to know more about you."

"Like what, for instance?"

God, she was bristly. Not about to give an inch. Maybe that was what intrigued him about her.

"Like where you come from, for instance. What kind of music you listen to. How you like your work. The real story behind that scar on your neck."

Stiffening, she speared her left hand into her hair and raked the blunt-cut ends forward. The gesture was instinctive, Cody guessed, and far more revealing than the terse reply she rifled out.

"Oregon. Soft rock. I like it very much, and I told you the story."

"You told me part of it. What you didn't tell me

was why you were consorting with the kind of idiot who rips beer cans in half with his teeth.''

She gave him a long, considering look. ''How about this, Doc? I'll tell you the details of that sorry incident if you tell me why you walked out on a six-figure job with one of the country's leading pharmaceutical companies and joined the Public Health Service.''

It was Cody's turn to stiffen. His decision to join PHS followed the worst months—and night—of his life. He would carry the guilt for that night for the rest of his life, but it wasn't something he wanted to share with anyone. Particularly this woman.

On the other hand, he'd asked the major to reveal a part of herself she was obviously reluctant to share. Fairness dictated that he do the same. Suddenly and inexplicably, he was annoyed that he still thought of her as ''the major'' and she referred to him as ''Doc.''

''The name's Cody,'' he said curtly.

''I know the name, but I don't think it's appropriate for me to use it given the fact you outrank me.''

''That holds when we're on duty. I went off the clock when I sat down on this table.''

So did she, but it took her a while to admit it.

''All right,'' she finally conceded. ''Tell me why you left your civilian job...Cody.''

He gripped the mug in both hands. ''My wife was

killed in a car accident. After her death, I needed a change.''

It was as simple as that, and so much more complex. His jaw clenching, Cody shut his mind to the bitter arguments and recriminations preceding the accident. But he couldn't blank out the horror that came after it.

''I'd been head of research at a major pharmaceutical company,'' he continued after a moment.

''Ditech,'' Jill murmured.

He nodded, not surprised. As chief of security, she would have read his background file.

''When Alicia died, I decided to opt out of the high-powered politics of pharmaceuticals and join PHS.''

''I bet your exit jolted a few folks at Ditech.''

''They got over it.''

More or less. Jack Conway would never forgive Cody for walking away from the company the old man had built from the ground up, any more than he'd forgive him for his daughter's death. Cody had learned to live with his father-in-law's unrelenting enmity along with the acid of his own remorse and regret.

''I've told you what you wanted to know,'' he said. ''Your turn.''

She hesitated, and for a moment he thought she would welch on their deal. She didn't.

''I was eighteen. A freshman in college. Too dumb

to leave the frat party when it became clear the guy I was with had drunk too much. So dumb I actually thought I should get him upstairs and into bed before he passed out or puked all over the place.''

She shook her head, making no effort to disguise her disgust with herself.

''I got him up to his room, but he didn't pass out. Instead, he hauled out another six-pack, popped a top and guzzled another beer.''

''At which point he ripped the can apart with his teeth?''

''Correct. He tossed the can aside and was reaching for another when I tried to leave.''

Cody went still, snared by that ''tried.'' He had a good idea what was coming before she picked up the thread of her story.

''He was too drunk to listen when I said no and too furious after I kneed him in the balls to pull his punches. I went down hard, landed on the jagged can, and almost sliced my own throat. The blood sobered him up fast,'' she added on a dry note. ''That, and my furious promise he'd finish his senior year in jail.''

''I hope to God he did.''

''He wasn't even charged. The campus cops got me to the hospital, where a blood test confirmed I'd consumed a few beers, too. The whole episode was chalked up to a lovers' spat that got out of hand.''

She downed the last of her coffee and slid off the table.

"I'm sensitive about the scar. I admit it. But don't think I don't learn from my mistakes. I took every self-defense course available on and off campus. I also switched my major to law enforcement. As a result, I'm working in a profession I love, have no qualms about taking on anyone, male or female, and, as a bonus, I get to wear the uniform of my country. In my more generous moments," she said with a sardonic twist of her lips, "I'm almost grateful to the bastard for crunching those cans."

Cody wouldn't go that far. He'd treated too many battered spouses during his internship and residency to feel anything but contempt for a man who would assault a woman. But in this particular instance, he couldn't help agreeing with the end result. Jill Bradshaw had made an ugly, potentially devastating situation into a major turning point in her life.

"Sounds like both our lives have taken a few unexpected twists and turns," he commented.

"Everyone's does."

"True. But not everyone winds up at a remote military site in the middle of the desert, surrounded by a quiet night and a whole lot of stars."

With a beautiful, intriguing woman just inches away.

He knew he shouldn't reach for her. Knew he shouldn't slide his hand under that smooth, silky hair.

If her blond brows had snapped into a frown, if she'd put up even the slightest show of resistance, he probably wouldn't have curled his palm around her nape and drawn her closer. For sure he wouldn't have bent his head and brushed his mouth over hers.

That was all he intended, anyway. Just a touch. A slow glide of lip along lip.

Maybe it was the way her breath hitched. Or the slow heat that collected in the skin under his palm. Whatever it was brought Cody off the table and onto his feet. Using his thumb, he tipped her head to a better angle and deepened the kiss.

Jill stood stock-still.

As the doc's mouth moved over hers, a jumble of emotions bolted through her. Her first instinct was to jerk away. Her second, to bring up her knee. He was too big, too strong, too damned good at this. Yet she remained still, testing herself, testing him.

To her surprise, she didn't experience so much as a dart of reluctance or distaste. His mouth and hands communicated only pleasure. Slow and tentative at first, faster and surer as his lips moved over hers.

With deliberate detachment she catalogued each sensation. The way he maneuvered into the kiss, with no awkward bumping of noses. The bristly scrape of his chin. The heat that transferred from his palm to her throat and all points south.

The hesitant, unsure, Goofy types she'd dated off and on over the years had never generated this much warmth so quickly. Okay, they'd never generated this much heat at all. She'd never let them. The fact that she wanted this kiss to go on indefinitely surprised the heck out of her and provided exactly the impetus she needed to break it. She stepped back, her muscles tensing, almost daring the doc to try to stop her.

He didn't. His hands dropped down to his sides and he looked almost as confused as she felt at the moment. She half expected him to apologize, was relieved when he didn't. Instead, he shagged a hand through his hair and dredged up a smile.

"Whew! I'm not sure where that came from."

Jill couldn't find anything to smile about. There was too much at stake.

"Wherever it came from," she said coolly, "it had better not happen again. We need to remember that we're here to do a job. A very important, very sensitive job. I suggest we both keep our minds on that and forget about this little time-out."

Time-out, huh? Cody figured that was as good a way to describe what just happened as any. He'd taken a momentary departure from common sense.

He'd shut himself away in a lab for too long, he decided as he walked the major back to the officers' trailers. Let his guilt eat away at him for too many months. He'd forgotten how it felt to share a quiet moment and a sky full of stars with a woman. And he'd sure as hell forgotten how something as simple and uncomplicated as a kiss could make his whole body sit up and take notice.

When his lips had covered hers, he'd felt the impact of her warm, seductive mouth in every muscle and nerve in his body. He was still feeling it, judging by the slight hitch in his walk.

Disconcerted by the jolt Jill Bradshaw had given his system, Cody left her at her quarters and retreated to his own.

Chapter 5

Pegasus arrived just past one the following afternoon.

By then Jill had conducted the morning guard mount, briefed her people on the snakebite incident, visited the dispensary to check on Sergeant Barnes and spent a good chunk of time on the horn with her counterpart up at Kirtland AFB in Albuquerque to confirm the size and composition of the security team that would escort Pegasus to his new stable.

A C-5 cargo plane flew the boxcar-size transporter into Kirtland just after nine. Once there, it was loaded onto a flatbed truck and escorted south. The convoy commander advised Jill when they were an hour out.

She notified Captain Westfall, who assembled his

key officers at the facility that would both house Pegasus and shield him from prying eyes in the sky. As the team waited in the cavernous hangar with mounting impatience and excitement, Jill skimmed a glance around the tight circle. They were all there, the leaders of the Star-Spangled Brigade: Captain Westfall, whipcord lean in his khakis; his second in command, Air Force Lieutenant Colonel Bill Thompson; Lieutenant Commander Kate Hargrave, her hair a bright red flame; Major Russ McIver standing ramrod straight and lantern-jawed like any good marine; Caroline Dunn, looking crisp and all business; Dr. Cody Richardson...

Her glance skidded to a halt, snagged by broad shoulders covered in khaki and the strong, tanned column of his neck. As if feeling her gaze on him, he looked her way. For a moment the memory of their kiss in the moonlight sizzled between them.

Deliberately Jill forced her attention to the civilians and enlisted personnel fanning out on either side of the officers. They were backed by test stands containing racks and racks of equipment. Pegasus would remain tethered to those racks until ready to run.

Jill's radio crackled, and her announcement that Pegasus had just been cleared into the test compound brought heads snapping up. The assembled group heard the rumble of the semi before it nosed around the hangar. Swinging in a wide arc, the vehicle backed up and stopped with the transporter just inside the open hangar doors.

The prime contractor's senior test representative crawled out of the semi's cab. A leather-tough, former Navy test pilot, he'd put Pegasus through his paces during the research and development phase. The fact that two of the three prototypes had crashed and burned probably accounted for the deep grooves bracketing the man's mouth, Jill thought.

The contractor was frantically assembling more prototypes, but urgent requirements had led the brass to press forward with operational test and evaluation of the one remaining vehicle. Pegasus's performance during this phase would determine whether or not the Department of Defense went ahead with its planned buy of the multimillion-dollar vehicle. Years of research and development were on the line here.

She held her breath as the boxlike transporter's rear doors opened and a long ramp slid out. Jumpsuited contractor personnel climbed inside the box to remove the restraints. A few moments later Pegasus rolled down the ramp.

"Doesn't look like much from where I'm standing," Kate Hargrave murmured.

Jill had to agree. She'd seen classified photos of the prototypes in different operational modes—churning up dirt, plowing through heavy seas, soaring above the clouds. This cigar-shaped pod with its bubble canopy and single tail fin bore little resemblance to those sleek vehicles.

True, it wore a coat of gleaming white paint on its composite, radar-evading skin. And the letters X-2, designating its status as a test vehicle, stood tall on its tail fin. Jill wasn't particularly impressed, though, until the contractor personnel hooked the vehicle up to generators and activated its systems.

A rear hatch slid open with a swoosh. The test pilot strode up the ramp and disappeared inside. Jill waited along with the others until his head appeared inside the bubble canopy. Suddenly doors lifted on two side narrow panels and Pegasus spread his wings.

"Whoa!" the Air Force rep exclaimed. "Look at that!"

The wings slid out with a whir, giving the vehicle a swept-back delta shape. A moment later, blades fanned out on the rear-mounted engines. Then it looked like a delta with propellers.

With another whir, the engines tilted upward. That position, Jill knew, would give the craft its hover capability. As captivated now as the rest of the cadre, Jill kept her eyes glued to the vehicle as its engines tipped back to a horizontal position. Contractor personnel wheeled support stands under the pod's nose and tail, then the pilot retracted the wheels. Pegasus settled gently onto the stand and took on the appear-

ance of a giant-size speedboat with twin propellers
just aching to find deep water.

"Oh, man," Caroline Dunn murmured to no one
in particular. "That baby looks like it will slice right
through heavy seas."

When the wheels lowered again, Jill was itching
to climb inside and see how the thing steered on
ground. First, though, Captain Westfall and the contractor's rep had to make the official transfer of test
responsibilities. Military photographers were on hand
to record the transfer, but no photos would appear in
the press. Like the Stealth bomber, this program was
being developed "in the black." It was Jill's job to
make sure that the bad guys didn't find out about
Pegasus until he galloped into their midst or swooped
down on them from the sky.

The simple transfer ceremony concluded with a
handshake and a flash of camera lights.

"Pegasus is all yours, Captain."

The contractor personnel would stick around to
contribute their expertise during the next phase of
testing, but Westfall would call the shots from here
on out. His first act was to lay a callused hand on
the white-painted hull, as if letting a skittish stallion
get used to his scent and his touch. His second was
to order the maintenance crews to paint the test
cadre's shield on the tail fin, just above the X-2.

"Let's head for the briefing room," he told his

officers. "I want everyone to brand the test parameters on their brains before we start putting Pegasus
through his paces."

The next few days sped by in a whirl of around-
the-clock activities. With Pegasus now on station, the
already tight security ratcheted up another few
notches. No one went in or out of the compound
without a thorough shakedown at each checkpoint,
and every tripped sensor triggered a full-out response.

Jill saw little of her roommates during those first,
hectic days. Even less of Doc Richardson. Good
thing, since she hadn't been able to shake the lingering memory of those moments in the moonlight.
Or answer the questions about the man that still hovered in her mind.

A cop down to her boot heels, Jill had done some
digging into Ditech, the company Richardson used
to work for. Odd that he still drove a vehicle leased
by Ditech. Odd, too, that he still retained a seat on
the company's board of directors. That smacked of
conflict of interest in her book.

She didn't get a chance to quiz him on the matter
until some days later, when she took her dinner tray
over to the group clustered at one of the tables in the
dining hall.

"Hey, roomie." Kate Hargrave scooted her chair
over a few inches to make room at the long table.
"Cari and I are beginning to think you're part vam-

pire. We rarely see her in daylight," she explained to the others.

"That's because you spend all your waking hours in the hangar testing the weather data fed into Pegasus's computers," Jill replied. "You'll see more of me when he slips his halter and gallops across the range. My troops and I will be galloping right alongside of him."

"Assuming you can keep up."

No way Jill was letting that million-dollar vehicle streak off across the desert without escort. "We'll keep up."

Smiling, Cari forked some of her vegetable lasagna and entered the debate. "That might be tricky. The run-ups on the tests stands have been impressive. If Pegasus performs out on the desert as well as he did on the stands, he'll leave everyone in the dust."

"We should make this a real horse race," Kate suggested, her green eyes gleaming. "Place a few side bets. Jill and her troops against Pegasus."

"I'm in," one of the others at the table said with a grin.

"Me, too."

"What are the stakes?"

Major Russ McIver's coffee mug hit the table with a thump. "This isn't a game, folks."

"No one said it was," Cari replied in her calm way. "We're just trying to lighten things up a bit."

Her answer didn't sit well with the stiff-shouldered

marine. "I'll lighten up when we've accomplished our mission. Until then, let's remember why we're here—which is *not* to run horse races."

Since Jill had uttered essentially the same sentiment to Cody Richardson just a few days ago, she could hardly disagree. Yet she found herself hiding a grin when the Coast Guard officer cocked her head. Jill had spent enough time now with her sister officers to get a good feel for why Caroline Dunn had been selected to command a heavily armed patrol boat. Despite her petite stature and quiet air, the woman took no prisoners.

Sure enough, the brunette leaned forward and gave the marine a polite smile. "I don't need reminding why I'm here. None of us do. You, however, need to remove that burr from your behind before it becomes so firmly lodged Doc Richardson has to perform a surgical extraction."

McIver's hazel eyes went agate hard, but before he could respond, a tall, dark-haired figure in khaki joined their small group.

"Was that my name I just heard mentioned?"

"It was," Cari replied.

"Who needs what extracted?"

"At the moment, no one, but we'll have to watch the situation closely and see how it develops." Pushing back her chair, she gathered her tray. "Here, you can have my seat. I'm done."

McIver's chair scraped the wooden flooring. He,

too, collected his tray. "You and I need to talk, Lieutenant. Let's take this outside."

Unconcerned, Cari wove a path through the tables. McIver followed hard on her heels. The doc stood watching them for a moment, then slid his tray onto the table and took the seat the Coast Guard officer had just vacated.

"What was that all about?"

"Just a little group dynamics in the works," Kate replied, her eyes alight. "Forget the horse race, gang. I'm putting my money on Lieutenant Dunn."

The conversation shifted back to the topic that consumed them all, which was Pegasus's first run. Jill savored her surprisingly delicious lasagna—she wasn't usually into vegetables—and listened to the various prognostications for success.

"Everything depends on the last round of diagnostics," Kate confirmed, checking her watch. "Dr. Santos, King of the Black Boxes, is supposed to run them this afternoon."

"I just left him," Cody commented. "He's set the final test for fourteen-thirty."

"Yikes!" Kate jumped up and grabbed her tray. "'Scuse me, folks. I want to go over the wind and air-temperature variables we plugged into the test program one more time."

Her departure started a general exodus, until only Jill and the doc remained at their end of the long table.

She refused to let her gaze linger on the crisp black hair curling just above the crewneck of his T-shirt. Or the strong, blunt-fingered hand holding his fork. Digging her own fork into her last bite of cheesy noodles, she downed the succulent morsel and was trying to think of a subtle way to introduce the leased Lincoln into the conversation when the doc took the lead.

"About the other night…"

"Yes?"

"Laying that kiss on you was way out of line. You were right. It can't happen again."

"I'm glad you agree."

She was. Really.

Still, it was one thing for her to put the skids on things. Another for the man to agree so adamantly they needed putting. Annoyed by a ridiculous little dart of pique, Jill shifted gears.

"Maybe you can clear up something that's been bothering me."

"What's that?"

"Your vehicle. It's still registered to Ditech."

He shot her a quick glance. "You ran the tags?"

"I did," she confirmed without a flicker of apology. "The first night, when I thought the vehicle had been abandoned out on the desert."

"And the fact that it's registered to Ditech bothers you?"

"You said you walked away from the corporation

to join the Public Health Service. I would have thought you'd walk away from the company perks, too.''

Carefully Cody laid down his fork. ''I resigned my position as head of Ditech's research department, but I still sit on their board of directors.''

''Isn't that a conflict of interest?''

''No.''

Cody had left the company, but he hadn't wanted to remove the clout that having someone with his credentials on the board provided. He'd owed Alicia and her father that much, at least.

Not that Jack Conway appreciated the gesture. Like his daughter, he refused to believe Cody didn't want the money, prestige or perks. George had never understood any act that wasn't driven by a profit motive.

From all appearances, Jill Bradshaw was having trouble understanding Cody's motives, as well. Leaning back in her chair, she studied him through a screen of thick, sun-tipped lashes.

''Let me make sure I've got this straight,'' she said slowly. ''The Public Health Service works for the U.S. surgeon general, who works for the secretary of health and human services, who in turn directs the Food and Drug Administration, which tests and approves the drugs Ditech produces. Yet you don't see that as a conflict of interest?''

''Neither do my bosses at PHS.''

"Why not?"

"One, I put my Ditech stock in a blind trust. Two, I included the full details of my board position when I filled out my financial disclosure statement. Three, I've been careful to remove myself from any issues or projects involving the corporation during my tenure with the Public Health Service."

"Hmmm. Just out of curiosity, Doc, who's the subcontractor for the nuclear, biological and chemical defense suite installed in Pegasus?"

She already knew the answer. Cody sensed it from the too-casual way she asked the question.

"Why don't you tell me?" he countered, his eyes narrowing.

"All right, I will. My research indicated it was a company called BioCorp, which underbid all its competitors for the Pegasus contract."

"Did your research also indicate Ditech was one of the competitors?"

"As a matter of fact, it did."

She leaned forward, not pulling any punches.

"The contract for the NBC defense suite for the three prototypes ran to well over a million dollars. If Pegasus proves its capabilities and goes into full production, we're talking hundreds of millions more."

Fury swept through Cody's veins, swift and icy. "What are you suggesting, Major? That I wormed my way into the Pegasus test cadre so I could invalidate BioCorp's system and give Ditech another chance to bid the contract?''

''I'm not suggesting anything.''

Yet.

The unspoken caveat hung between them, as heavy as an unsheathed scimitar and twice as lethal. Cody almost felt the damned thing hovering over his head, a breath away from his neck.

Christ! So much for thinking he and Jill had sparked a small flame the other night. Or that it needed dousing. Obviously, the heat had all been on his side.

That shouldn't put such a kink in his gut. Nor should the major's probing questions. She was only doing her job. He knew that, accepted it. Yet couldn't shake his anger. Shoving back his chair, he picked up his tray.

''Look, Major, you attend to the security for this project…''

''I will,'' she said evenly.

''…and I'll attend to the NBC suite.''

He fully intended to exit on that note, but an urgent call swung him around.

''Doc!''

One of Cody's corpsmen shoved through the door to the dining hall and forged a path through the troops still finishing their lunch.

''We need you at the clinic ASAP.''

Cody dumped his tray back on the table. "What's the problem?"

"We've got a patient who presented with dizziness, severe headache and aching muscles. His temperature's off the charts."

"Sounds like the flu. Who's the patient?"

"A civilian. Dr. Santos. He's one of the test engineers."

"Hell! Santos was fine when I left him a while ago."

"He's not fine now. He says it hit him all of a sudden. Came on with the force of a sledgehammer. He could barely stagger into the clinic."

Jill felt her own stomach knot as Cody joined the medic and hurried out of the dining hall. Dr. Ed Santos wasn't just "one" of the test engineers. He was the *senior* test engineer for the entire project. If he went down sick, the test schedule could well take a hit.

Less than a week into the project and it was sounding as though Pegasus might have hit its first major snag.

Chapter 6

D<small>r.</small> Santos *did* go down sick, and the Pegasus test schedule *did* take a hit.

Word from the clinic was that Ed Santos had picked up what looked like a particularly virulent bug. His temperature continued to spike at dangerously high levels throughout that day and into the evening. Doc Richardson sent blood and urine samples by chopper to the lab at the Kirtland AFB Hospital for testing.

Ed's backup scrambled to cover both his and Santos's responsibilities, but the final diagnostic run didn't take place until the following day. Concern for the genial test engineer tempered the team's satisfaction with the excellent results. Like a high-strung stallion held in check at the end of a leading rein, Pegasus was put through his gaits via black boxes, and all systems were checked.

Ed's fever finally broke late that evening. The officers assigned to the cadre held an impromptu celebration to celebrate the good news about Ed and the success of the diagnostic run-up. After a week of living almost in each other's pockets, they were beginning to bond into a tight, cohesive unit. Even Russ McIver, their resident stiff-necked marine, unbent enough to join the group congregated at the picnic tables located between the trailers.

Kate provided the pretzels, tortilla chips and salsa from her seemingly bottomless supply of goodies. Bill Thompson, the Air Force rep, brought the beer. Cari and Jill raided the dining hall for soft drinks and a garbage sack of ice.

Captain Westfall surprised everyone by showing up in gray jersey jogging shorts and a T-shirt with U.S. Navy emblazoned across the front in gold letters. As best Jill could recall, this was the first time the tall, spare officer had exited his quarters wearing something other than his uniform.

When he appeared in their midst, the small group of officers jostled knees and elbows to jump to attention. Westfall waved them back to their seats.

"As you were. We're off duty until morning."

Only until morning, when Pegasus would finally

slip his leash and take his first gallop across the desert.

"I just visited Ed Santos," Westfall told the group. "He's looking a whole lot better than he was last time I saw him."

"Any idea what hit him?" Bill Thompson asked.

"The doc still thinks it was some kind of virus, although he won't know for sure until he hears from the lab up at Kirtland."

"Speaking of the doc," Kate said with a nod toward the clinic, "looks like he's finally going off duty, too."

Jill shifted her glance to the khaki-clad figure making his way toward them through the hot August dusk. The sudden trip to her pulse annoyed the heck out of her. She should be used to Cody Richardson's chest-squeezing, rib-knocking impact by now. And she shouldn't be surprised that his gaze traveled over the group and stopped dead on her.

His expression held none of the anger it had yesterday, when she'd challenged him on his ties to Ditech. Nor did his eyes hold any hint of warmth. They were neutral. Completely neutral.

That was fine with Jill. She couldn't afford to mix business with pleasure any more than the doc could. Which didn't explain why her mind noted completely irrelevant details like the small ducktail in his black hair when he dragged off his hat.

"Here, Cody," Kate said. "We'll scrunch up and make room for you."

"I'm fine standing. I'll just grab a beer."

"There's plenty of room."

Hips bumping, Kate nudged Bill Thompson to the far end of the bench. Jill had no choice but to move along with Kate. Cody settled beside her, careful not to make contact, and tipped his beer.

Jill shut her mind to his nearness and listened as the group got down and dirty with the technical details of tomorrow's run. Above them, the New Mexico sky slowly darkened with towering purple clouds that glowed bright neon pink on the bottom. A slash of lightning forked down from one dark pillar and stopped the conversation cold. A rattle of thunder followed some seconds later.

"What's the forecast for the next twenty-four hours?" the captain asked Kate when the echo died. She'd briefed him and the rest of the cadre earlier, but he wanted assurance the clouds piling up like stacks of dirty laundry would pass as predicted.

"I checked again right before I came outside. Thunderstorms in the area until midnight. Clear skies tomorrow."

Westfall nodded, relaxing.

"Actually, I think we're about to experience one of New Mexico's dry storms," Kate said with an eye to the rapidly approaching clouds. "The air is so parched and hot, the rain will evaporate before it hits the ground.''

Her prediction proved correct, but the absence of raindrops splattering against the dirt didn't lessen the storm's spectacular fury. Within moments the sky off to the west was bursting with pyrotechnics, thunder boomed like an artillery fusillade, and wind began to whip up the sand.

''Time to move things inside,'' Kate said, flipping the plastic lid on the salsa. ''Someone grab the beer and chips.''

Hands reached for the bags and cans while Kate beat a hasty retreat to the women's quarters. The others followed, but Jill waylaid Captain Westfall before he joined the rest.

''Can I talk to you a minute, sir?''

''Sure.''

She threw a glance at the departing group and waited until Cody's broad shoulders disappeared inside the mobile unit with the others.

''It's about Doc Richardson,'' she said, turning back to the captain. ''Do you know he once worked for Ditech Corporation?''

''Yes, I do.''

''And that he still sits on their board of directors?''

''Yes, again. Richardson included the information in his financial disclosure statement.''

''It doesn't concern you that he's on the board of a company that lost out on its bid to supply the nuclear, biological and chemical defenses for Pegasus?''

"It did," Westfall confirmed with a nod, "until I decided there was no one more qualified to test that suite than Cody Richardson. If there's a flaw in Pegasus's NBC defenses, he'll find it. I *want* him to find it. No way I'm going to send our troops into a situation where they might face chemical or biological agents unless I know the vehicle conveying the men will protect them.''

"How can you be sure Dr. Richardson won't manufacture a flaw to invalidate the system?''

The captain's steel-gray gaze lasered into her. "Sabotage the project so Ditech will get the contract, you mean?''

Jill didn't flinch. The S-word sounded flat-out ugly said aloud, but it had to be voiced.

"Yes, sir, that's what I mean.''

"I can't be sure," Westfall admitted. "Any more than I can be sure you won't go berserk and crash your Humvee into Pegasus when we take him out for his first field test tomorrow.''

That possibility hadn't occurred to Jill, nor did the captain appear to take it all that seriously.

"Since I put the doc through the same grilling I did you before I approved either of you for this project, I've got to go with my gut. Richardson isn't going to sabotage the project, and you aren't going to crash your Hummer.''

"Let's hope not," she muttered, considerably re-assured by his prior knowledge of Cody's connection to Ditech. For the first time since their confrontation in the dining hall yesterday, she let herself relax.

Kate's built-in antenna picked up the subtle change in her roommate almost the moment Jill and the captain came inside and rejoined the others. She arched a brow, but refrained from comment.

Cody, on the other hand, appeared more tense than he had outside. He stood apart from the group, a cell phone glued to his ear. Brow furrowed, he nodded once before snapping the phone shut and making his way over to Captain Westfall.

"That was the lab at Kirtland Hospital. They've isolated the bug that attacked Ed Santos. It appears to be a new strain of flavivirus."

"And that is?"

"A genus of pathogens that include the yellow fever, dengue fever, Japanese encephalitis, and the hepatitis C virus. Kirtland is going to send the sam-ples over to Decker Research Lab there in Albu-querque to identify the actual serological character-istics. Luckily, Decker is right next to the base. It's one of the few labs in the country that possesses the reagents from human volunteer studies required for a specific diagnosis."

"How serious is this bug?"

"It depends on its serology. The Center for Dis-ease Control maintains a database that lists more than five hundred registered viruses. Some, like yellow fever and dengue, can lead to death in severe cases. Others barely raise a rash or a sniffle.''

"Well, we already know this strain packs more of a wallop than that.''

"Yes, we do. What puzzles me is where Ed picked it up. Hepatitis C is usually spread through contaminated body fluids, but other members of the flavivirus genus are usually transmitted by arthropods like mosquitoes and ticks. This dry, desert air breeds damn few of those.''

"Maybe Ed was infected before he arrived on-site.''

"Could be, although most symptoms usually manifest themselves within a few days of contact. Just to be on the safe side, I'm going to have my folks spray the compound and test our water and food supplies for possible contamination.''

"Sounds good, Doc. Let me know if you find anything that concerns you.''

"Will do.''

The impromptu party broke up not long after Cody's departure. Jill needed to make a final check with Rattler Control before hitting the sack but helped Kate and Cari clean up first.

"So what's happening with you and the doc?'' the irrepressible weather officer asked as she dumped empty cans into the trash. "I got the distinct impression you two have cooled your jets a bit."

"There are no jets to cool."

"Right. And I suppose that kiss you conveniently neglected to tell us about never happened."

Jill turned to stare at her. "How do you know about that?"

"I told you, sweetie, I have my ways."

"The woman's a walking satellite dish," Cari put in drily.

Kate accepted the backhanded compliment with a little bow. "Back to you and the doc. You aren't going to tell us you didn't lie awake thinking about that smooch?"

"Nope, I'm not going to tell you that. Or anything else concerning the doc and me."

Kate made a face, but accepted the rebuff with her sunny good nature.

Jill went back to work scooping up crumbs. She wouldn't admit it, but Kate was right. She hadn't been able to get that darned kiss out of her mind. Mostly because she kept trying to decide why she'd derived such pleasure from the experience. Cody Richardson wasn't her type. He was too big, too sure of himself, the sort who usually raised her instinctive hackles.

Maybe that was it, Jill thought as she crushed the tortilla chip bag and tossed it into the trash. Richardson kept throwing her off balance, first by their encounter out in the desert, then by ignoring the proceed-at-your-own-risk signs she put out whenever a man got too close. Maybe she was confusing her cop's instincts with a prickly female intuition that Cody represented trouble.

And maybe she should just put the man out of her mind and concentrate on the mission! The interior of their quarters restored to some semblance of order, Jill went back out into the stormy night.

As Kate had predicted, the day of Pegasus's first field test dawned impossibly clear, as only mornings in the New Mexico desert can. The entire test cadre had converged on the hangar by eight. By nine, Pegasus had emerged from his stall into the dazzling sunshine and was ready to run. His wings remained folded back to form a narrow delta, the propellers tucked out of sight. With his tubular body, bubble canopy and upright tail fins, he looked more like a rocket on wheels than a racehorse.

Jill and her troops would accompany Pegasus on his first run, but not in ATVs. With a supersecret, multimillion-dollar prototype to protect, she and her crews were going out fully armed.

Sergeant Greg Barns was at the wheel of Jill's Hummer. Fully recovered from his tussle with the rattler, he positioned their Humvee behind and to the left of Pegasus. The second security crew angled their Hummer to the right. Both armored vehicles bristled with a full complement of arms. One was equipped with a roof-mounted TOW missile launcher on a rotating circular ring, giving it a 360-degree field of fire. The other had a 50-caliber machine gun. A similarly armed chopper would provide coverage from the sky.

Heat rose from Pegasus's white-painted composite shell in shimmering waves when Major Russ McIver and Bill Thompson climbed through the side hatch. They both wore special fire-retardant flight suits in gray-green Nomex. An embroidered American flag patch was Velcroed to each of their left shoulders, the Pegasus test patch to the right. After a systems check and engine run-up, Mac gave a thumbs-up to the ground crew. The crew pulled the chocks, Mac throttled forward, and Pegasus began to roll.

The Hummers rolled right along with it. For the first few moments, anyway. Then Pegasus kicked up his heels. With a whoosh that stirred a cloud of sand, he streaked off across the desert.

"Whooee!" Sergeant Barnes stomped down on the accelerator. "Look at that baby go!"

Clenching her teeth against the bone-rattling ride, Jill divided her attention between the vehicle ahead, continual sweeps of the landscape all around and the special test monitors installed on the Hummer's dash. The monitors tracked Pegasus's speed, direction, radar profile, heat signature and exhaust emissions, among other variables. Larger, more precise monitors provided the same data to the cadre following the run back at test ops.

With fierce concentration, Jill listened through headphones to the communications between Mac and the test engineers. Dr. Santos was still too weak to man the controls, but his backup was covering well.

"We have you at forty percent forward thrust, Pegasus."

Mac's reply crackled through the headset. "Confirming forty percent."

Jill and Greg Barnes exchanged glances. He had his boot flat against the floorboards, and they could barely keep up, yet Pegasus hadn't even broken into a sweat.

"Prepare to dispense detection countermeasures."

"Roger, Control."

Mac and his copilot ran through a short checklist and signaled they were ready to dispense the high-tech chaff.

"Proceed, Pegasus."

Eyes narrowed, Jill strained against her seat harness and kept her gaze locked on the swiftly moving vehicle some hundred yards ahead. Suddenly it disappeared, lost in a cloud of minute silvery particles that caught the sun's glare and threw it back in blinding flashes of light. According to the specifications, the tiny particles could suck light from the atmosphere even on rainy, overcast days and produce almost the same effect.

"Damn," Barnes muttered. "I can't see a thing."

Jill's glance whipped to the monitors. They showed nothing but green fuzz. Her jaw tight, she keyed her mike.

"Test control, this is Rattler One."

"Go ahead, Rattler One."

"We've lost visual contact and our screens are blank. We're terminating chase immediately to avoid possible collision with the test vehicle."

"Confirming termination, Rattler One. Pegasus, conclude countermeasures test and return to base."

Jill didn't draw in a full breath until the blinding glare dispersed and she had Pegasus in her sights again. There he sat, a good half mile away. Heat shimmered off his hide and she could swear the damned thing wore a smug, just-try-and-catch-me grin.

The entire test cadre was waiting inside the hangar when Pegasus ambled back into his stall. The engineers were jubilant. Kate Hargrave flashed her most brilliant smile. Captain Westfall gave Mac and Bill Thompson a grin and a hearty thump on the back. Even quiet, reserved Cari Dunn treated the marine to a nod of approval.

Only Cody Richardson seemed to be missing. Jill removed her helmet, swiped back her sweaty bangs and searched the hangar. Climbing out of the Hummer, she made her way to Cari's side.

"Where's the doc?"

The Coast Guard officer threw a look around her. "Beats me. He was in the ops center with the rest of us for the test run."

Kate joined them and, of course, supplied the answer. "He went back to the clinic to check on Ed Santos."

Jill nodded and put the doc out of her mind while Captain Westfall conducted the initial post-run debrief. A more detailed review would follow after the test engineers analyzed the data they'd collected.

The session concluded, she and her troops left the hangar and headed for Rattler Control, where Jill conducted her own debrief. Her security forces were both elated by Pegasus's success and sobered by the realization that they'd have to work like hell to keep up with him in the ensuing tests.

"Particularly when he takes to the mountains," Jill emphasized, circling that run on the test schedule. The mountain run was still some three days off, but the prospect of scrabbling after Pegasus when he charged up the steep, craggy slopes had her rethinking the deployment of his escorts.

She'd have to position teams halfway up the mountain in advance, have them pick up the chase if Pegasus left the crews tailing him in the dust.

"We'll put Rattler Four here," she decided, marking the spot on the map. "Rattler Five a little higher up."

"We might want another team at eight thousand feet," her top sergeant suggested, studying the topographical map. "It's outside the test parameters, but after what we saw today, the engineers might just give Pegasus his head and see how high he can climb."

Jill concurred, so preoccupied with revising the security annex to the test plan that it was some hours before she realized Cody Richardson wasn't anywhere on-site.

Chapter 7

Jill first learned Cody had left the site from one of the gate guards coming off shift. His activity report included the information that Dr. Richardson had passed through his checkpoint at 11:22 this morning.

"He left the compound?"

"Affirmative, ma'am. He passed through the second checkpoint a half hour after clearing mine."

"Did he indicate his destination?"

"Not to me."

Frowning, she stuck her head inside the control room. "I need a lock on Dr. Richardson's ID."

The MP manning the desk pulled up an electronic map of New Mexico and entered the code for Cody's ID. Assuming the doc had the holographic card on him, the sensor embedded in the thin plastic would pinpoint his exact location. If he didn't have the ID on him, Jill thought grimly, he'd have some serious explaining to do when he returned from wherever he'd gone. Her muscles cording, she waited while the MP zeroed in on a blinking red dot traveling north on I-25.

"I read him just about fifty miles south of Albuquerque, Major."

"Thanks."

Jill raised Captain Westfall on her communicator. The tension seeped out of her when the CO confirmed he'd authorized the doc's trip to Albuquerque. Evidently the researchers at Decker Labs were having difficulty identifying the virus that attacked Ed Santos. It didn't match any of the currently known strains. Since Pegasus would remain in his stall for the next few days while the test engineers pored over the data from the first run, Doc Richardson had requested permission to drive up to Albuquerque and offer his expertise to the researchers at the lab.

"I think you should make a quick trip up there, as well," the captain added. "I'm told the security forces at Kirtland have specially modified their Hummers to give them more speed in this type of terrain. You might want to take a look at what they've done."

After today's performance, there was no question the chase vehicles could use more acceleration.

"You can chopper up and back," the captain said. "Or drive back with the doc when he returns tomorrow."

"I don't think I'll need that long to check out the mods."

"Take the time, Major. Have dinner at a good restaurant. Hit the mall. You haven't been off-site since you arrived with the advance contingent three weeks ago. A change of scene will do you good."

Jill had to admit the prospect of chowing down someplace other than the dining hall held definite appeal. As good as the cooks here were, she'd kill for a plateful of spicy New Mexican green-chili cheese enchiladas or a big, greasy hamburger.

"You can hook up with Doc Richardson at the Kirtland Inn and arrange transportation back," Westfall said. "He indicated he's staying there tonight. I'll talk with you after you return, Major."

"Yes, sir."

A call to flight ops indicated they could have the chopper assigned to the site ready to fly by the time she arrived at the helo pad. She made another call, this one to Kirtland. The 377th Security Force Squadron's operations officer agreed to meet her at the flight line and give her a hands-on demo of his unit's equipment.

Hurriedly she went over the schedule for the next twenty-four hours with her flight chiefs, deputized her top sergeant to stand in for her at any post-test meetings and threw a few things in an overnight bag.

Forty minutes later, the chopper touched down at Kirtland. The sprawling base sat in the shadow of the Sandia Mountains. It was home to a number of organizations, including the Air Force Inspection Agency, Sandia National Laboratories, and the Nuclear Weapons Directorate tucked away on the far side of the base. Jill knew the security screens protecting the nuclear site were every bit as elaborate as those protecting the Pegasus site.

With a word of thanks to the crew for a smooth ride, she grabbed her bag and jumped out. Ducking under the still-whirling rotor blades, she darted across the tarmac to the vehicle waiting beside Base Operations. All around her the busy flight line bristled with the aircraft assigned to the 58th Special Operations Wing—specially configured Blackhawk helicopters, the old, reliable H-1N Huey helos like the one Jill arrived in, fixed-wing C-130 Combat Talon aircraft, and the tilt-engine CV-22 Osprey.

Jill gave the Osprey a particularly intense once-over. The newest aircraft in the military inventory, it combined a helicopter's hover capability with the speed and long distance of fixed-wing flight. Pegasus took that unique technology and added the ability to operate on the surface of the earth and under the sea, as well. If the test vehicle proved itself, and the program went into production, several dozen Pegasus clones would no doubt sit on this same runway in the not too distant future. If it didn't—

Jill cut that thought off at the pass. She wasn't going to think about the millions of dollars in research, development and test that would be lost. Not right now, anyway.

Squinting in the bright glare of the late-afternoon sun, she greeted the major whose folks had responsibility for security and transport of the supersecret weapons developed, tested and stored at Kirtland.

"Thanks for agreeing to meet with me on such short notice."

"No problem." He flashed her a grin from behind a pair of aviator sunglasses. "We love to strut our stuff. Hop in and I'll give you the twenty-five-cent tour."

By the time the major pulled into the 377th Security Force Squadron's motor-pool area an hour later, Jill was practically salivating. She'd equipped her detachment with the latest, state-of-the-art equipment, but the sheer size and lethalness of this unit would turn any cop green with envy.

She spent another hour with the wizards who'd modified the 377th's vehicles. She left with a computer printout of the tech order and a promise of immediate delivery of enough parts and equipment to take care of her small fleet.

The slowly sinking sun was painting the mountains to the east a watermelon pink when the major dropped her off at the Kirtland Inn. The spectacular view riveted Jill for a few moments, until a glimpse of a midnight-blue SUV a few parking spaces over claimed her attention. Her gaze on the Lincoln, Jill started for the office and walked smack into the khaki-clad figure just exiting the building.

Cody reached out, steadying her with a firm hand on her arm. Surprise flitted across his face before his black brows slashed down into a frown. "What is this, Major? Are you keeping me under surveillance?"

Evidently he hadn't forgotten their last conversation.

"If I did have you under surveillance," Jill replied calmly, "I guarantee you wouldn't know it."

"Then why are you here in Albuquerque?"

She glanced around, saw no one was within listening range. Still, she couched her reply in terms that made no reference to Pegasus. "I wanted to check out some modifications the base security forces have made to their escort vehicles."

Suspicion still lingered in his blue eyes. "So it's just a coincidence we both drove up the same day?"

"Actually, I flew up, but the chopper had to return to base. The captain suggested I drive back with you tomorrow."

"Did he?"

The suspicion was still there. Jill saw she'd have to work to regain the ground she'd lost with the doc.

"Yes, he did. He also suggested I treat myself to dinner at a local restaurant. Care to join me? If you don't have any other plans, that is."

"I haven't made other plans," he said slowly, almost reluctantly. "But I need to swing back by Decker Labs afterward. They're running some special tests for me and should have the results later this evening."

"Fine by me. You're already checked in, I see. How about I do the same and meet you here in a half hour?"

Cody used the half hour to shower off the dust and heat of the August day. Rasping a hand across his chin, he decided he might as well scrape off his five-o'clock shadow, too. Luckily he'd thrown some jeans and a white shirt in his overnight bag along with a clean uniform shirt. He hadn't intended to turn this trip into an excursion, but certainly wouldn't mind blending into the background as an ordinary civilian for a few hours.

When he exited the Visiting Officers Quarters and made his way to his vehicle, the mountains to the east formed a dark, jagged silhouette against an indigo sky. To the west, the sun was about to drop into the Rio Grande. The mesa above the river was an impossible blaze of red, pink, gold, and purple. The temperature had dropped to a comfortable ninety degrees or so, made bearable by the total absence of humidity in the air. Cody leaned against the fender of the Lincoln and let his gaze roam the darkening sky.

As it had the first night he'd arrived in New Mexico, the incredible panoply of stars tugged at something deep inside him. With the universe spread out like that, a man should be able to put things in perspective. Like his life. His work. His guilt.

He waited for the regret and remorse to stab at him with their usual sharp-honed blades, but the cuts didn't go as deep as they usually did. To his surprise, he had trouble picturing Alicia's furious face the night of their last argument. Instead, the image of a strong, determined chin, gold-flecked brown eyes, and a smooth sweep of wheat-colored hair kept edging Alicia's aside.

Well, hell! Here Cody had spent the first half of the four-hour drive up to Albuquerque telling himself he had to get Jill Bradshaw out of his head. He'd spent the second half trying to figure out how the heck she'd burrowed in so deeply. He'd known her for just over a week, had been on her ten-most-wanted list for almost that long. He was still carrying the scars of a stormy marriage that ended in tragedy. He didn't need to tangle with another woman all too ready to believe the worst of him.

Yet he couldn't shake the memory of Jill's mouth

under his. Or the urge to slide his lips down the column of her throat and kiss away any lingering pain from the scar *she* kept hidden under her sleek, shining hair. Frowning, he shoved his hands in his jeans pockets and scowled at the night sky.

That was how Jill found him some moments later. Ankles crossed, shoulders hunched, indulging in a serious bout of stargazing. *Another* bout of stargazing.

He didn't appear to be deriving a whole lot of enjoyment from the exercise. His jaw had set to a rigid line and the muscles of his forearms were taut beneath the rolled-up sleeves of his white shirt. He turned at the sound of her approach, his tight expression relaxing.

''Ready?''

''Ready.''

Sweeping a glance over her jeans and scoop-necked white tank top, he opened the door for her. She had to use both the hand grip and the raised running board to boost herself into the high-riding Lincoln. Sinking into buttery soft buckskin, she surveyed a dash that seemed to contain as many dials and screens as her Humvee.

Cody walked around the front of the vehicle and took the driver's seat. He was like his vehicle, she thought, slanting him a glance as he hooked his seat belt. Built tough and handsomely packaged.

Okay, she could admit the truth when it whapped

her right between the eyes. Despite her usual aversion to big, muscled types, there was something about the doc that set her nerves to humming. All it proved was that she wasn't dead from the neck down.

"How does Mexican sound?" he asked, keying the ignition.

Jill's stomach leaped in delight. "Mexican sounds good. *Very* good."

"The folks at Decker Labs recommended a restaurant not too far from the base," he told her, angling an arm across the back of her seat to twist around and look through the rear window before backing out of the tight parking spot. "I'm told the place doesn't look like much on the outside, but serves the hottest salsa in town."

"I can handle it."

He flicked her a glance. For the first time since their discussion in the dining hall, his eyes held something close to a smile.

"Yeah, I bet you can."

When he withdrew his arm, his rolled-up cuff riffled Jill's hair. Little pinpricks of sensation raced down the back of her neck.

"Good Lord!" she gasped some twenty minutes later, "your friends at the lab got it wrong. This stuff isn't hot. It's subatomic!"

Eyes watering, she fanned her mouth with one hand and snatched up her iced tea with the other. She downed half the glass before she doused the fiery conflagration started by one innocent tortilla chip and a scoop of hot sauce.

"I've eaten a lot of Mexican food before," she commented, "but nothing like this."

The waiter had warned them New Mexico's summer chili crop was just reaching peak potency, but she hadn't expected anything quite *this* hair-raising. When Cody ladled up a heaping scoop and crunched contently, Jill eyed him with new respect. Not so much as a single drop of sweat popped out on his brow.

"You must have a cast-iron stomach."

"As a matter of fact, I do." He grinned around another heaped chip. "I spent some time in Guatemala doing research a few years ago. Everyone on the team came down with an intestinal irritation at least once except me. I ate the produce, feasted on chiles relleños and chicken pepian, and polished every meal off with bananas in a chili-spiked chocolate sauce."

"The local cuisine sounds…interesting."

The laugh lines crinkling the corners of Cody's eyes were even more interesting. He slouched back against the high-backed booth, relaxing in her presence for the first time. The restaurant lights gave his hair a blue-black sheen. The sides were trimmed close to his head in good military style, but not even the ruthless cut could tame the hint of a wave on top.

He looked good in civvies, she had to admit. Almost as good as he looked in uniform. Unfortunately. Deciding this was as good a time as any to learn more about the man behind the uniform, Jill copied his slouch and slumped back against the booth.

"Tell me more about Guatemala. I've pulled temporary duty in Colombia and took a side trip to Peru, but haven't hit the Central American isthmus yet."

"Guatemala is one of the most beautiful places on earth," he said simply. "It's the heart of the Mayan world, with the Pacific on one side, the Caribbean on the other and everything you can imagine in between. Scruffy deserts, sky-scraping volcanic peaks, a rain forest so thick we had to hack our way back down a path we'd cut just eight or ten hours previously."

"How long were you in the country?"

"Three months. We spent most of it in the central highlands west of Guatemala City."

"Doing research, you said?"

"Right."

And trying to sort through the mess he'd made of his marriage.

Cody dropped his glance to his iced tea. Idly, he traced a fingertip down the condensation clouding the glass. Alicia had been furious when he'd decided to head the team flying down to Guatemala. He was Ditech's senior medical researcher, for pity's sake! A member of their board of directors. He didn't need to trek out to some godforsaken little village in a backwater country and pick up who-knew-what bacteria. Cody's reminder that bacteria happened to be his business had only added fuel to the fire.

Three months apart hadn't cooled Alicia's anger. She'd been armed and ready for him when he walked back in the house, and hadn't let up until the rain-soaked night he finally returned fire. The day after that, she was dead.

"What kind of research?"

Deliberately he focused on the woman across from him. Her warm brown eyes and steady gaze drew him from the dark pit of his memories.

"We were testing a new ultraviolet water purifying system. Hurricane Mitch left half the country's population without safe drinking water. It also left them without electricity. The purifier Ditech devised could be powered by a car battery or a sixty-watt solar cell. Passing water through the system's UV light filter inactivated the DNA of pathogens and sanitized water at a cost of about five cents U.S. per one thousand gallons."

"Is that good?"

"Very good."

For Ditech as well as for Guatemala, Jill guessed, but the waiter's arrival with two monstrous platters ended the conversation. The next few moments were taken up by an explanation of each item on the overflowing plates and another warning to go easy on the hot sauce. The ensuing half hour was devoted to enchiladas so spicy they burned a hole in her esophagus, pinto beans that seared the roof of her mouth and repeated refills of both her iced tea and water glasses.

"I never realized I possessed such masochistic tendencies," she commented, surveying her near-empty platter. "I'm stuffed. Burning from the inside out, but stuffed."

"Hope you saved room for a sopapilla. Doused in honey, it'll put out some of the fire."

As if on cue, the waiter appeared to spirit away their plates and replace them with a basket of puffed dough squares still warm from the oven.

"You're right," Jill said after the first bite made a slow descent to her tummy. "The honey helps."

Tearing off another corner of the sugary bread, she squeezed on a generous dollop, popped it into her mouth, and chewed contentedly. Across the table, the laugh lines appeared beside Cody's eyes again.

"What?"

"You've got honey dribbling down your chin."

Oh, nice! Nothing like displaying her couth or lack thereof. Jill daubed at her chin with her napkin and only succeeded in smearing the sticky stuff.

"Hold still," the doc ordered, leaning across the table. "I'll get it."

Jill surrendered her napkin, which he dipped in her water glass. She also surrendered her chin. He curled a hand under it and tipped her face to the light. His thumb grazed the side of her jaw, making a small circle while he worked. The cloth felt damp and cool against Jill's skin, Cody's touch disturbingly warm and erotic. She managed to keep her expression neutral, but it took some doing.

He must have felt something of the tension snapping along her nerves. His brow creasing, he withdrew his hand and dropped the napkin.

"I think I got it all. You finished? I need to stop by Decker Labs before it gets too late."

Chapter 8

Jill saw an entirely new side to Cody at Decker Labs.

She'd fixed his Public Health Service officer persona firmly in her mind. If asked, she could describe in precise detail his uniform cap with its anchor and caduceus, his knife-creased khaki shirt and pants, even the white lab coat and the stethoscope he draped around his neck while seeing patients at the clinic. On-site and at work, he was cool, calm and in charge.

She'd also observed him twice in civvies, first when she'd put him facedown in the dirt and now tonight. Each time he'd left a definite impression. Under oath, Jill would have to admit Cody Richardson could certainly do justice to a pair of jeans.

At the research center only a few blocks from the restaurant, she discovered another facet of this confusing, confounding man. To the folks at Decker, he was apparently a god.

"Decker is a relatively small lab," he informed her as he pulled into an almost deserted parking lot. The Lincoln's headlights swept across the facade of a two-story tan stucco building decorated with turquoise trim and prehistoric Indian symbols. "They're doing some interesting studies on the nasal and respiratory irritation of Gulf War veterans."

Nasal irritation didn't sound like a particularly vital research area to Jill until Cody elaborated.

"We're just beginning to understand the long-term effects of blowing sand and the inhalation of intense hydrocarbons from the oil fires during Operation Desert Storm. Preliminary findings indicate the constant irritation could have weakened the nose-brain barrier."

"That doesn't sound good."

"It isn't. The theory is the weakened barrier allowed particles of the depleted uranium used in armor-piercing artillery shells to enter the central nervous system of soldiers in the field. We know DU is toxic to the kidney because of its properties as a heavy metal. The research is attempting to determine if it's neurotoxic, as well."

Desert Storm had kicked off during Jill's senior year in college. She'd missed that action, but a num-

ber of the soldiers in the Pegasus detachment were
Gulf veterans. That concerned her. So did the fact
the military still fired the shells Cody had referred
to.

"The Army's been using depleted uranium armor-
piercing shells for years," she said as she slid out of
the cloud-soft leather seat. Thudding the car door
shut, she joined him for the short walk to the front
door. "So have civilian law enforcement agencies.
Are you saying researchers are just now discovering
DU particles can be inhaled?"

"Not in most situations," he replied, pressing the
buzzer beside the double glass doors. "But the combination of smoke from those oil field fires, blowing
sand and extensive use of DU weaponry made for
very unique circumstances. What's being studied
now is whether that combination *could* have contrib-
uted to the variety of symptoms Gulf War veterans
reported after the conflict."

Jill was a little slow making the connection, but
when she did, her stomach knotted. Blowing sand.
Armor-piercing artillery shells. The only thing the
Pegasus project lacked was a fire that billowed thick,
black smoke. So far!

Impatiently she waited until a security guard had
buzzed them in, checked their IDs and called for an
escort. Drawing Cody to the towering ficus that dom-
inated the lobby, she asked the question now burning
in her mind.

"Do you think the unique circumstances you mention might have something to do with this mysterious bug Ed Santos picked up?''

Cody cast a cautious look at the guard and lowered his voice. ''Do I think he inhaled it? No, I think he either ingested it or was bitten by an insect that transmitted it. But until we identify the strain and the source, I'm not ruling anything out.''

Oh, great! As if Jill didn't have enough to worry about with two hundred square miles of desert to defend against intruders and a multimillion-dollar weapon system to safeguard! Resisting the impulse to gnaw on a fingernail, she waited with Cody under the drooping ficus.

''Dr. Richardson.''

The researcher who came forward to greet them wore three-inch spike heels, a black silk sheath that clung to her slender curves and a silver necklace with a turquoise-studded squash blossom the size of Manhattan under her white lab coat. More turquoise and silver banded her wrists and dangled from her earlobes.

''I'm sorry I missed you this afternoon. I hope my people took good care of you.''

''They did.''

Returning her warm handclasp, Cody introduced Jill to Dr. Sylvia Nez. The sleekly beautiful director of Decker Labs acknowledged the introduction with a friendly nod, but her fellow scientist clearly claimed her full attention.

"I was on my way to a gala at the Santa Fe opera when my people called with the results of the second round of tests. I had to come back and verify the findings myself." Her dark eyes glinted. "They're pretty exciting."

An answering gleam leaped into Cody's eyes. "Are they?"

"We think you've discovered a new strain of fla-vivirus. Its RNA and genomic nucleic-acid structures are similar to the Ntaya and Rio Bravo agents, but it has its own distinct serology."

She led the way down a hall bathed with light so bright the glare off the tiled floor almost hurt Jill's eyes. Some doors stood open, revealing offices with furnishings buried under piles of books, medical journals and reports. Other doors were closed and prominently marked with Restricted Access in large red letters.

Dr. Nez halted before a pair of doors near the end of the hall. As her long fingers worked the cipher lock, she gave Jill an apologetic glance over her shoulder.

"I'm sorry, Major Bradshaw. We don't have your credentials or your clearances on file. You'll have to wait in the prep area with one of my assistants."

"No problem."

"Robert will take care of you," she said, indicating an earnest young technician. "Get the major some coffee, will you, Rob?"

"Sure." The assistant's gaze turned almost worshipful. "How about you, Dr. Richardson?"

Declining with a smile, Cody followed Dr. Nez through another set of doors. The lock clicked shut behind him. The young technician swallowed his obvious disappointment at being left out of the action and filled a foam cup.

"Do you take cream or sugar?"

"Neither, thanks."

He handed Jill the cup and gave the closed inner door another glance, this one filled with reverence.

"I can't believe I actually got to meet the man who developed the current universal protocols for immune electron microscopy."

Whatever that was.

"I understand Dr. Richardson is a big dog in his field," Jill commented, intrigued by the research assistant's awe.

"Big! Cody Richardson is *top* dog as far as I'm concerned. I just about fell out of my chair when Dr. Nez called to say we were going to run some tests for him. Then, to have him show up at the lab in person this afternoon. Wow!"

Hooking a chair, he dragged it around to straddle the seat. Jill took a cautious sip of the scalding brew while the intense young man catalogued Cody's many notable achievements. Rob was running out of steam when he let drop a comment that brought Jill's head up.

"Everyone thought Ditech would go belly-up when Dr. Richardson left," he said. "Good thing for them he retained his position on the board."

"Why's that?"

"Ditech invested heavily in research they hoped would lead to an inexpensive, readily available antianthrax vaccine. Unfortunately, the research was seriously flawed. Dr. Richardson convinced the board to terminate the project before the staggering costs dragged the whole company under. Over his father-in-law's strenuous objections, or so the rumor goes."

Carefully, Jill set the cup aside. "His father-in-law?"

"Right. Jack Conway, founder and CEO of Ditech. Dr. Richardson was married to his daughter."

Well, hell! So much for Jill's investigative skills! Despite her several inquiries into Cody's background, she'd failed to turn up that particular tidbit.

Not that it really changed anything, she supposed. Cody had disclosed his financial dealings with Ditech. The Department of Defense investigators who'd checked the doc out would have made the connection to the company's CEO prior to granting him his security clearances. Still, Jill filed the interesting bit of information away for follow-up when she returned to the Pegasus site.

If she ever returned to the Pegasus site. Four cups of coffee and two trips to the ladies' room later, she was beginning to wonder if Cody had taken up residence at Decker Labs. Finally he and Dr. Nez emerged from the inner sanctum. The aura of excitement that enveloped them was almost palpable.

"Sorry this took so long," he said, not looking the least penitent. "Ready to go?"

She managed not to comment that she'd *been* ready for the past hour. The beautifully groomed director of Decker Labs opened the outer doors for them, but left it to Rob to escort the visitors to the exit.

"We'll forward the samples to the National Institute of Health and the Center for Disease Control," she promised. "Unless you want to make the notifications yourself."

"Your folks should do it. They were the ones who ID'ed this baby."

"With your guidance! Brilliant work, Dr. Richardson."

Grinning, Cody tipped her a two-fingered salute. "Back at you, Dr. Nez."

The goggle-eyed Robert looked from his boss to his idol, but was too well trained to pepper either of them with questions about the specific findings. He picked up on their vibes, though, and fairly shimmered with excitement as he escorted the visitors out. They'd barely passed through the guard's checkpoint before Rob dashed back down the hall.

"So?" Jill asked as she and Cody stepped out into the star-studded night.

"We've identified the strain. It's definitely a variation of the flavivirus. A particularly virulent variation, judging by Ed Santos's symptoms. I still don't know how or where he picked it up, but at least now I know exactly what I'm looking for."

His voice vibrating with the exultation of a big-game hunter who'd bagged a rare trophy, he took her elbow to steer her toward the Lincoln. A woman of Jill's size and expertise in martial arts didn't particularly need steering, but she decided not to point that out.

Her reluctance to shake off his hold had nothing to do with the needles of sensation shooting straight from her elbow up her arm. Nothing at all. She just didn't want to put a damper on his triumph by emitting her usual prickly, hands-off signals.

For exactly the same reason, Jill didn't shut the door in Cody's face when he accompanied her to her room at the Kirtland Inn some fifteen minutes later. He was obviously too keyed-up over this new bug he'd discovered to hit the rack. After four cups of coffee, so was she.

He didn't wait for an invitation to follow her inside the suite. Decorated in glowing desert colors, the rooms boasted oak furnishings, a plush mauve carpet and opaque glass light fixtures engraved with the same Zia sun symbol that adorned New Mexico's state flag.

As she closed the door and turned to survey Cody, though, the room's decor was the last thing on Jill's mind. That was pretty much taken up by a large, restless male. *His* mind, obviously, was still on his bug.

"I haven't decided what to name it," he told her, frowning as he straightened the brochures and phone books on the desk. "The various strains are usually named after the place they first show up."

"Hence Ntaya and Rio Bravo?" Jill guessed.

"Hence Ntaya and Rio Bravo," he confirmed. "There's also the Japanese Encephalitis group, the Modoc group and the Uganda S. group."

"Sounds like that little sucker gets around."

"It does."

He moved to the well-stocked minibar and realigned the wineglasses on the shelf above the counter. Hiding a grin at his obvious need to do something, *anything,* to release his pent-up excitement, Jill folded her arms and leaned against the wall beside the door.

"So what's the problem here? Why can't you name your variation 'Albuquerque'?"

He left off fiddling with the wineglasses and threw her an impatient glance. "Because it hasn't presented in Albuquerque. Not as far as we know, anyway. It showed up some two hundred miles south of here…at a highly classified site no one's supposed to know about."

"Oh. I see your point."

The scientist in him was obviously as frustrated as he was thrilled by his find. He raked a hand through his hair, carving four neat furrows in the black pelt.

"I told Dr. Nez and her people that I was doing some research for Public Health Service on communicable diseases in the southwest when one of my team members took sick. They wanted to know exactly where, but I dodged the question by telling them the team has been highly mobile and we weren't sure where my colleague picked it up."

"That part's true."

"Right now." His blue eyes drilled into her. "If any more of our folks become infected, though, I'll have to report it to the Center for Disease Control. I'd also want access to local health records to make sure we're not dealing with a potential epidemic."

Jill gulped, uncrossed her arms, and pushed away from the wall. If they *were* dealing with a possible epidemic, preserving the security and secrecy of the Pegasus site would become an almost impossible task.

He must have read the dismay in her face. Shaking off his utter absorption with his find, he crossed the room to where she stood. "The Center for Disease Control is part of Public Health Service," he reminded her. "If we have to, maybe we can keep this all in-house."

"Yeah, maybe."

The glum reply pulled Cody from his total immersion in the night's findings. Without thinking, he slid his hand under Jill's hair and rested his palm on the warm, smooth skin of her nape.

"Hey, we should pop the cork on some champagne and celebrate. It isn't every day a guy gets to add a new entry in the Bad Bug Book."

She'd stiffened at the contact, but his comment drew a curious look. "Bad Bug Book?"

"Actually, it's the U.S. Food and Drug Administration's *Handbook on Pathogenic Microorganisms and Natural Toxins,* but that's too heavy even for those of us in the business."

"Is that so?"

She tipped her head back, spilling a silky curtain over Cody's wrist. He stared into brown eyes fringed by gold-tipped lashes. For the second time in the space of a few hours, he took a kick right to the gut. This one, he noted with the clinical detachment of a scientist, was considerably more powerful than the wallop he'd experienced at Decker Labs.

Then Jill ran her tongue along her lower lip, and Cody's clinical detachment went to hell. All that remained was the urgent, greedy desire to kiss her again.

"Forget the champagne," he muttered, his gaze fixed on that wet, glistening stretch of skin. "I've just figured out a better way to celebrate."

This was crazy. Jill knew it, sensed Cody knew it,

too. She had no business standing here like a brain-less Barbie doll, waiting all gooey-eyed for Ken to dip his head. Yet that's exactly what she did.

She expected him to kiss her, was ready for the heat, the punch. But nothing in their previous contact prepared her for the electric jolt when he took her lower lip between his teeth. The slow, erotic nips generated shiver after shiver.

She was just getting used to the shuddering sen-sation when he soothed the sensitive skin with a warm, wet sweep of his tongue. Afterward, Jill could never quite remember whether she wrapped her arms around his neck to draw his head down or he took the initiative. However it happened, they ended up with her shoulder blades pressed hard against the wall again and his mouth hot on hers.

Jill gave fleeting thought to her mission, to the need to maintain distance, to good ol' Goof and the gawky, gangly types she'd tried so hard to convince herself she preferred. The truth hit her about the same time Cody sandwiched her between the wall and his muscled body. She wasn't afraid or intimidated by his strength. She delighted in it. For obscure reasons she didn't stop to analyze, his masculine power stirred some atavistic feminine response deep within her.

On that thought, her conscious mind shut down. As greedy now as he was, Jill arched her spine to increase the sensual friction of his hard contours against her thighs, her belly, her breasts. When her hip made contact with the bulge pushing at the zipper of his jeans, Cody dragged his mouth from hers and slammed both palms against the wall beside her head.

"If we're going to stop this celebration," he ground out, "we'd better do it now."

He was giving her the choice. Jill swallowed, agonizing for all of ten or twenty seconds before blowing out a ragged breath. "I vote we continue the celebration and see where it takes us."

"I can tell you right now where it'll take us," he warned. "Are you sure that's what you want?"

"Yes. I think."

"That's not good enough," he said with a rough rasp in his voice. "I'm not your beer-guzzling college date. I won't take what you're not ready to give."

"I know exactly who you are. And I'm getting more ready by the second. Now, just kiss me, dammit."

Chapter 9

Cody complied with Jill's irritated command and kissed her.

Once with finesse. Once again with somewhat less skill and considerably more greed. He couldn't seem to get enough of her eager mouth. Or her body. It strained against him and set fire to his nerves at every major contact point.

When she hooked a heel around his calf to increase the pressure even more, Cody went from hungry to seriously hurting. For the first time in three years, he didn't stop to think, didn't force himself to remember. Sliding his palms down the stuccoed wall, he cupped Jill's rear and canted her hips into his.

All too soon even that intense sensation wasn't

enough. Gritting his teeth, Cody dragged his head up once more. ''We keep this up and I won't be able to stagger upright into the bedroom.''

Her head tipped back as far as the wall would allow. Cody's pulse pounded at the heat staining her cheeks. She wet her lip again, almost stopping his heart in his chest, and gave a husky choke of laughter.

''Who says we have to go into the bedroom?''

''Good point.''

With one bunch of his muscles, he hoisted her up until her legs locked around his hips. One turn and three steps took him to the oak-trimmed sofa. They hit the cushions in a tangle of arms and legs.

As his weight crushed her into the cushions, a momentary panic pierced the pleasure spiraling through Jill. The instinct to ball her fists and jerk up her knee ripped through her, only to die an instant death when he brushed back her hair and dropped a soft kiss on the puckered scar.

''If I ever come face-to-face with the bastard…''

She held her breath as his lips traced the ridged line from her neck to her jaw.

''…who did this to you…''

His mouth was hot on her flesh, his hands fumbling for the hem of her tank top.

''…he'll be eating through a straw for a long, long time.''

''That's interesting,'' Jill managed to say breathlessly, raising her shoulders to let him drag off the top. "I told him essentially the same thing. He pretty much kept out of my way after that."

Cody didn't answer. She wasn't sure he'd heard her. His glance was riveted on her breasts, only half-covered by a scrap of lilac nylon trimmed with ivory lace. He tugged at the lace and dropped a string of kisses on the rounded slopes, but didn't make any comment until he'd unsnapped her jeans. When he'd dragged them down to reveal matching bikini panties, he raised pleading eyes to hers.

"Please tell me you don't wear this kind of underwear with your BDUs."

"These or some very similar. A girl's got to express herself, even in BDUs. *Especially* in BDUs."

Groaning, he buried his face in the curve of her stomach. "I'll never be able to look at you in uniform again without wondering what you're wearing under your top layers."

His breath was hot and damp against her belly. Jill hollowed her stomach under his nipping little kisses.

"As a matter of fact," she returned, trembling under the assault, "I'm wondering the same thing about you right now."

Grabbing a fistful of his collar, she tugged him up until she could reach the buttons on his white shirt. She was wedged against the cushions, half under him, half squashed against the sofa back, but managed to pop the buttons and slide her hands inside.

Her palms glided over what seemed like acres of soft cotton T-shirt before finding the bare skin of his upper arms. Warm and tightly corded, his muscles jumped under her touch.

If she was going to call a halt to things, it had to be now, before either of them shed any more clothes. Jill knew it. Recognized that the responsibility for what happened next lay squarely on her shoulders. The ripple of warm flesh under her hands stirred such a fever of impatience and hunger that she accepted the responsibility eagerly. For tonight, for this crazy slice out of time, she intended to shut down her mind and just feel.

Cody must have sensed her inner decision. Or her hunger. Or both. Angling off the sofa, he rolled to his feet with the casual grace of an athlete. Any other time, that smooth coordination of bone and muscle might have bothered Jill. Not now. With her mouth throbbing from his kisses and her skin suddenly cool where it had been deprived of his heat, she wanted him naked and fast.

Thankfully, he wanted the same thing. He stripped down to his shorts. Before tossing his jeans down to join his shirt, he dug his wallet out of his pocket. Jill got a brief glimpse of the condom he extracted from his billfold and dropped on the table beside the couch.

She had protected herself against pregnancy since college days. She wouldn't leave that to chance. But

the cautious side of her nature, the cop side that had
seen too much misery and darkness, took fierce satisfaction in knowing Cody didn't leave such matters
to chance, either. When he turned back to her, Jill
got a glimpse of wide, muscled shoulders, a chest
dusted with black hair, and long, lean flanks. He bent
a knee and wedged it between hers, skimming a
glance down her sprawled body. "Something tells
me I'll be having erotic dreams about lilac and lace
for a long time to come."

Not just about lilac and lace, Cody thought wryly.
He had a hunch he'd be spinning late-night fantasies
about every inch of this woman, in and out of uniform. His blood pounding, he reached for the front
hook on her bra.

Lord, she was beautiful! He took a moment to admire high, firm breasts tipped a dusky rose before
sliding his hands under the small of her back. Arch-
ing her up toward him, he let his mouth roam her
belly, the tender undersides of her breasts, her nip-
ples. By the time they were knee to knee and chest
to chest, her breath was coming hard and fast and
Cody was damned near bent double with the need to
have her.

Panting, she reached down between their bodies
and slid her palm inside the waistband of his Jockey
shorts. He grunted as her fingers closed around him.
Every muscle in his body strained with the urge to
drag her back down to the cushions, but he forced

himself to wait, to let her prime him until he had to clench his jaw against the pumping, pulsing sensations.

Then it was his turn. Burying one hand in her hair, he ravaged her mouth while his other hand found the damp heat between her thighs. He slid a finger inside her slick channel, followed with another, and used the heel of his hand to exert a light, grinding pressure.

Within moments, she was wet and gasping. Moments more, and she flung her head back. A high flush stained her cheeks. Her eyes were wide and hot.

"Cody! I don't... I can't..."

"I can't, either," he growled.

He was all thumbs as he fumbled for the condom. Sheathed and so hungry for her he abandoned any attempt at skill or finesse, he tumbled her to the cushions. She parted for him eagerly, welcomed him with a clench of her muscles that had him gritting his teeth.

He almost lost it after the first couple of thrusts. He managed to hang on to his control, if not his sanity, until Jill arched her back and groaned. He felt her tighten around him again, felt the wild shudders of her climax and, somehow, held back until the torrent slowed to mere ripples.

Only then did he flex his thighs, drive in and lose himself in her.

* * *

"Am I too heavy?"

"Unnn."

The unintelligible grunt was the best Jill could manage.

"Sounds like a no," Cody muttered, nuzzling her tangled hair. "God, I hope it's a no. I don't think I have enough left in me to move for another hour or so."

Since she was sprawled under his very limp and very heavy body at that moment, Jill sincerely hoped he'd overstated the situation. Despite being pinned to the sofa cushions, though, she made no effort to dislodge him. Nor did she feel so much as a flutter of unease at her vulnerable position. She was too sapped to feel anything at all.

She drifted in and out of pleasure, breathing in the salty tang of perspiration and sex. The combination was intoxicating beyond words. Sighing in hedonistic pleasure, she trailed a forefinger down the bumps on his spine. That stirred him enough to go from nuzzling the top of her head to folding down so he could nibble on her ear. She hunched a shoulder in a vain attempt to escape the tickling wash of his hot, damp breath.

"That was a fast sixty minutes," she grumbled, not quite ready to abandon her boneless lethargy.

"It was, wasn't it?"

The smug pride in his reply stirred a giggle deep

in her throat. Of all the reactions Jill had expected to experience after the most shattering climax of her life, laughter wasn't one of them. She would have let the giggle float free if a sudden, insistent prod at the inside of her thigh hadn't diverted her attention.

"Cody?"

"What?"

"You may have regained your strength, but I haven't."

"Not to worry." His voice was low and rough as he folded his body like a pretzel and reached for his wallet again. "I'll do all the work this time."

Jill made some inarticulate protest, which, thankfully, he ignored. Mere minutes later she was spinning through another universe again.

She woke to the sound of pelting water and a satisfied male singing decidedly off-key.

Pulling her face from the depths of her pillow, she dragged up both sandpapery eyelids and crooked her head toward the bathroom. The door was shut, but the steam escaping from underneath confirmed he was in the shower.

Her glance shifted to the digital clock on the night-stand—6:20 a.m. Groaning, Jill dropped her face back into the pillow.

They'd migrated to the bedroom sometime during the night. She wasn't exactly certain when. She was pretty sure the relocation came after her second, mind-shattering climax and sometime before the third.

The man was inexhaustible.

Jill hugged the pillow, a smile playing at the corners of her mouth. And here she'd shied away from big, athletic types all these years. There was definitely something to be said for strength, stamina and muscle control.

But not when it came packaged in an individual she had to work with for the next few months. One she still couldn't quite get a handle on.

Sighing, Jill rolled onto her back and let the clear, slicing light of morning cut through her sensual haze. She'd done some dumb things in her life. Not walking out on her drunken date back in college ranked right up there at the top of the list. She only hoped last night wouldn't take second position.

By the time Cody strolled into the bedroom wearing only a smile and a towel wrapped low around his hips, she had the sheet tucked up under her arms and her back propped against the headboard. She was determined to play it cool, but the sight of the man fresh from the shower almost had her swallowing her tongue. His damp hair stood up in gleaming black spikes. Missed droplets of water glistened on his shoulders. One rivulet trickled down to lose itself in the dark swirls of hair on his chest.

Oooh, boy! Jill wasn't used to so much masculinity this early in the morning. Or any other time of the day, for that matter. Clearing her throat, she greeted him with what she hoped was casual nonchalance.

"Good morning."

He came across the room, planted one hand on the headboard and delivered a long kiss. Not having had the benefit of a toothbrush, Jill kept her lips locked together. Even close-mouthed, she felt the slow burn all the way to her tightly curled toes.

"Now it's a good morning," he said in a satisfied tone.

"Uh, Cody, I think we need to talk."

"Yeah, I figured that was coming. How about we talk over breakfast? I'm starved." He straightened and gave her a crooked grin. "I don't know about you, but I worked up a hell of an appetite last night. I'll get dressed while you hit the bathroom."

Still damp and sleek as a panther, he headed for the other room to find his clothes. Jill stayed pinned against the headboard, staring at the strip of untanned skin displayed just above his sagging towel.

Well, that was interesting. *We need to talk* was usually a killer lead in. It certainly hadn't seemed to concern Cody. Or surprise him. Thrown off balance by his nonchalance, Jill trailed the sheet behind her and headed for the bathroom.

They opted for breakfast at the Kirtland Officers' Club, situated only a short walk from the transient quarters. Jill slid her tray along the chrome rail and treated herself to a toasted bagel and orange juice. Cody once again demonstrated his ironclad stomach by choosing huevos rancheros and greasy fried potatoes.

"How can you guzzle hot stuff for dinner *and* breakfast?" she muttered, eyeing the beans, minced onions and green chilies topping his eggs.

"When in Rome…" he replied with a shrug. "How about that table over there by the window?"

She navigated to the spot he indicated and caught her breath at the vistà framed in the floor-to-ceiling windows. Peachy-brown and sharp-etched in the morning sunlight, the Sandias rose to form a jagged ridge against a cloudless sky.

Cody emptied his tray, took hers, and placed them both on a handy nearby holder. They downed their first caffeine of the day in silence. Their systems jump-started, Jill munched on her bagel while he dug into his slithery, sloppy eggs.

"Okay," he announced after a couple of healthy bites, "let's hear your list of reasons why last night wasn't a good idea. Or do you want me to do the honors?"

"The floor's all yours," she replied, curious to hear what he had to say.

"All right." He took another swig of coffee, set his cup aside. "One, it was an aberration, a case of getting carried away by the thrill of a scientific discovery.''

Jill had been carried away, all right, but not by the discovery of a new bug.

"Two," he continued, "we let our glands overrule our good sense. Three, we'll be working together for the next few weeks and need to maintain a professional protocol that's hard to project when all we're thinking about is jumping each other's bones. Four, we hardly know each other. Five…"

He paused and let his glance slide over her face.

"Five?" Jill prompted.

"You're still not sure about me."

When she didn't deny it, he sat back and hooked a brow. "Did I miss any of the major issues?"

"Nope, I think you hit them all."

Except the fact that the insides of her thighs still tingled from whisker burn. She shoved aside the memory of Cody's face buried between her legs and met his sardonic gaze.

"You know everything I just mentioned is bull, don't you?"

"Pretty much," she admitted. "Whatever the heck is going on between us, it doesn't seem to respond to logic or lists."

"So what's the plan?" he asked, lobbing the ball neatly into her court. "Where do you see us going from here?"

Wishing she had an answer to that question, Jill

pushed the remaining half of her bagel around the plate with the tip of a finger. She wasn't the coy type, wouldn't string Cody along if she wanted to, which she didn't. Neither could she deny that they'd kicked down some walls in the past eight hours that could prove hard to rebuild.

"I don't know *where* we go from here," she answered, "except back to the site."

"And forget what happened last night?"

"No." Honesty compelled her to admit the truth. "Last night was...unforgettable."

"Good. I'd hate to think I was the only one who thought it was the hottest sex this side of the planet Mars. You rocked me right off my heels, Bradshaw."

If he was off balance, Jill sure couldn't tell it by the way he put away the rest of his eggs and fried potatoes. Two cups of coffee later, they were on their way back to their small, dusty corner of New Mexico.

Jill was surprised by the long stretches of companionable silence they shared as the Lincoln cruised south on I-25. The Albuquerque skyline soon dropped out of sight, as did the Isleta pueblo with its mission church standing square against the morning sun. Then came the flatlands of Bosque Farms and the rich Belen valley, cut by the meandering Rio Grande. Soon the green fields gave way to the dusty brown of Soccoro and a bronze plaque announcing that they'd just entered the Jornada del Muerto.

"The journey of the dead," Jill relayed when Cody pulled over for her to read the wayside sign. "The roughest and deadliest part of the Camino Real, which ran from Mexico City to Santa Fe. With no water, no grazing and no wood for cook fires, this was ninety miles of pure hell."

Looking out over the immense empty desert, she could believe it.

"Wonder why the Camino Real didn't just follow the river?" Cody mused.

"It says here the Rio Grande changed course after almost every major storm, leaving behind high ridges, deep gullies, and treacherous bogs of quicksand. Despite the dangers and the constant threat from hostile Apache, travelers made better time on flat, dry land. Those who finished their journey, that is."

Cody hooked a wrist over the leather-wrapped steering wheel. His eyes hooded, he surveyed the bleak terrain. "It's going to be interesting to see if Pegasus finds this land as unforgiving as the Spanish caravans did."

Jill nodded, remembering that the northwestern tip of their secret site bordered the Jornada del Muerto. Pegasus would take his first swim at the south end of this deadly strip, in the deep, silent waters of El-ephant Butte. First, though, he had to conquer the mountains spearing up out of the desert far to the east.

"Considering the success of his initial run," she said, eyeing those rugged peaks, "my bet is Pegasus kicks butt."

Cody flicked her a glance. "Let's hope so."

"Yeah," she echoed softly. "Let's hope."

Chapter 10

Jill spent the next two days in a whirlwind of activity.

As promised, the Kirtland cops sent the necessary equipment to modify her unit's Humvees. The genius in charge of the site's motor pool supervised the installation. Her MPs checked out the mods by making runs into the mountains to preview the route Pegasus would take.

During one run, they stumbled across a car parked at the end of an almost inaccessible dirt road. The vehicle sat beside a trickling stream. The patrol approached cautiously, weapons drawn, and scared the hell out of the couple frolicking naked in a shady pool formed by a basin of rocks.

The startled and highly indignant male was ID'ed as the son-in-law of the county sheriff. As it turned out, the overly well-endowed brunette who scrambled into her clothes was *not* the sheriff's daughter. Responding to the scene, Jill kept her expression neutral.

"You realize this is a restricted area?"

More worried now than indignant, the male half of the illicit twosome palmed a hand over his slightly balding crown. "Yes, I know but…"

"But what?"

"We've never seen any evidence of military activity in this area before."

"Come up here often, do you?"

"No, no! Not, uh, often."

Nervously he swatted at the gnats buzzing around his damp hair. At this elevation, the ecology of rugged rock and thick pines formed a sharp contrast to the seemingly barren desert at the base of the mountains. The air was cooler here—and populated with more annoying insects.

Jill explained the sudden appearance of a heavily armed patrol with a vague allusion to military exercises being conducted in the area. The illicit lovers weren't interested in military activity, only in covering their tracks.

"Look, you don't have to file a report or anything, do you?"

"No."

"So we can go?"

She wasn't worried these two would spread the word about a beefed-up military presence in the area.

"You can go."

Naturally, the incident provided great fodder for jokes back at the compound. Jill closed her ears to the ribald comments she overheard her MPs tossing back and forth, but couldn't resist sharing a chuckle with Kate and Cari later that evening.

"Wish I'd been there when my troops first arrived on the scene and ordered him out of the pool," she said when the three women congregated for a rare gathering. As busy as they all were, they'd seen each other only in passing since the impromptu party after Pegasus's first run.

"According to the report, the man was buck naked," Jill related with a grin, "and hopping from one bare foot to the other on the scattered pine needles."

"From what I hear," Cari drawled, "your troops barely spared him a glance. Word is his girlfriend's bra size was at least a 36-double-D. Or maybe that was her IQ. I've heard several different versions of her response when asked to explain what they were doing in the area."

Jill sputtered with laughter. "She said they were just cooling off. I won't tell you how my guys responded to that."

Kate wasn't quite as amused by the episode as the

other two. "I hope they both got pine needles stuck somewhere other than the soles of their feet. What is it about marriage that turns some men into complete jerks?"

Too late Jill remembered Kate's philandering ex. She exchanged a look with Cari, who responded to the question with a shrug.

"Beats me. Although I've met one or two who didn't require marriage to qualify for jerk status. I can think of one in particular right here."

"Let me guess," Kate said, her scowl giving way to a grin. "He wouldn't happen to be a United States Marine, would he?"

The usually placid Coast Guard officer rolled her eyes. "If I hear 'that's not how we do it in the corps' *one more time*…"

Restored to her normal sunny self, Kate chuckled. "So now there are two of you striking sparks off your fellow cadre members. Although…" She turned her curious gaze on Jill. "I've noticed a definite lessening of hostilities between you and the doc in the past few days. Did something happen up in Albuquerque you want to tell us about?"

"Nope."

"Nope, nothing happened or nope, you don't want to tell us?"

"No comment."

"Come on, girl, give! You and Cody depart the site separately, not exactly on friendly terms, and return together the next day in noticeably more mellow moods. What's a roommate to think?''

Jill would hardly describe her mood the past few days as mellow. The wild night in Cody's arms released the sexual tension that had built between them from their first kiss. Unfortunately, the mere thought of that night generated an entirely new batch. With some effort, she banished the memory of his bristly five-o'clock shadow scraping along the slopes of her breasts.

''What a roommate *should* think,'' she told Kate firmly, ''is that her colleague discovered a new strain of virus and was justifiably pleased by it.''

''Uh-uh. That won't work. I'm a scientist, too, remember? I was the first on our team to pick up evidence of a solar flare a few years back, but I don't recall that it put a hitch in my stride. Which,'' she added, throwing up a hand to forestall Jill's protest, ''is exactly what happens whenever Cody walks into a room and spots you.''

Well, at least the aftereffects weren't all one-sided. Now if Jill could just decide what the heck she wanted to do about them.

She was still trying to make up her mind when she stepped out into the predawn darkness the next morning. Anticipation bubbled and fizzed in her veins. Pegasus would tackle the mountains today. Jill wanted to go over the composition of the escort teams and dispatch two to the higher elevations well ahead of the test run.

She had just rounded the corner of the prefab unit that served as the women officers' quarters when the door opened to the unit that was two over from hers. Jill's stomach did a quick roll when she recognized the khaki-clad figure silhouetted in the light spilling through the door. Deliberately she slowed her step. Cody wasn't the only one with a hitch in his stride, she thought ruefully.

"'Morning, Doc."

Coming out of the darkness, her greeting caught him by surprise. He spun in her direction and relaxed his taut shoulders only after spotting her in the shadows.

When he came down the steps and closed the short distance between them, it was Jill's turn to go tight all over. She guessed from his smile what he intended before he curled his hands around her upper arms and dragged her against his chest. His head came down, his mouth closed over hers, and she forgot every prohibition against public displays of affection while in uniform.

When he raised his head, her breath came in short, embarrassing pants. So did his, she noted thankfully.

"I've been aching to do that since we got back from Albuquerque," he growled.

She could hardly deny the truth when it had pretty well slapped them both in the face. "Me, too."

"I saw the lights on in your quarters last night. You have no idea how close you came to getting a visitor."

"I've got two roommates," she reminded him, refusing to think about what Kate would have made of a late-night visit from the doc.

"So do I," he said ruefully, gliding his hands up and down the stretch of skin left bare under the rolled-up sleeves of her BDUs. "Helluva note when grown adults have to sneak out in the dark to neck."

If she hadn't been so distracted by the river of goose bumps he was raising on her arms, Jill might have pointed out that neither of them had sneaked anywhere.

"Speaking of the dark," she said instead, "what are you doing up so early?"

"I was lying in bed thinking of you when I decided to do another search of the Center for Disease Control's database."

"I suppose it's logical you've linked me to a database of diseases in your mind, but I have to admit it doesn't exactly do a whole lot for the ol' ego."

"It should," he countered with a grin. "You've worked your way in my system, Bradshaw. Just like the bug that got to Ed Santos."

"And you honestly believe that line will score you points with women?"

"Make that singular," he said slowly, his grin fad-

ing. "You're the first woman—the only woman—
I've tried to score with since my wife died."

Whoa! She hadn't seen that coming.

The quiet declaration added another layer to the
tension simmering just under her skin. The attraction
was still there, the shivery, sensual delight he generated with each touch, the whispered promise of
pleasure to come. Suddenly that anticipation took on
a deeper hue, a different heat.

Thrown off balance, Jill struggled to come up with
an appropriate response. Her confusion must have
shown on her face. Cody's grin came back with a
vengeance.

"You don't have to look so surprised. I've pretty
well spent the past three years in a lab. Your closest
competitors have been germs."

She seemed to recall Kate mentioning a media
consultant back in Virginia who'd like to sink her
hooks into the man but decided this wasn't the time
to introduce a third party into the conversation. A
fourth party, she amended, remembering his reference to his wife.

"I need to hit the computers," Cody said, bringing
his mouth down to hers once more. "I'll see you at
the hangar for the pretest briefing."

He intended a quick farewell, a last taste to take
with him to his tiny office at the clinic. He should
have anticipated the swift punch to the gut that hit
him every time he kissed this woman.

His timing really sucked, he thought as they headed in different directions. Both he and Jill were involved in a mission essential to national defense. The last thing either of them should have on their minds was sex. Yet all he had to do was feel her mouth under his and his entire body went on red alert. Hell, who was he kidding? He didn't need a taste. A mere glimpse of her honey-colored hair or trim, tight behind got him hard.

He'd told her the flat-out truth a few moments ago. Like the virus that had hit Ed Santos, Jill Bradshaw had worked her way into Cody's system. She was in his head, in his blood.

Grimacing at his less-than-poetic phrasing, he unlocked the door to the clinic and flicked on the lights. With Santos back on the job and no other patients to tend, the small dispensary had reverted to standby mode. The hospital corpsman assigned to the site would report to the hangar to provide medical coverage during the test, as would Cody.

First, though, he wanted into the Center for Disease Control database. He'd already searched it for recently reported cases of illnesses with unidentified causes and symptoms similar to Ed's. Now that Decker Labs had reported the specific serological characteristics of this new strain, though, the CDC computers might have matched it with other cases across the country.

Luckily, every workstation in the clinic was

equipped with high-speed, encrypted laptops that would access just about every reputable medical database. The Pegasus site was too remote and the clinic staff too limited to rely solely on their collective knowledge. These sleek little computers put the entire medical universe at their fingertips.

A universe, Cody discovered after a half hour of determined searching, that apparently didn't include any outbreaks of high fever, dizziness, and nausea caused by the same bug that had hit Ed Santos. Blowing out a long breath, he shut down the computer and left the clinic.

The warm, dry night was fast giving way to a hot, dry dawn. Cody angled a glance at the mountains to the east. The slopes were still black as pitch, but the jagged peaks were backlit by spears of red and gold. In a few hours Pegasus would race toward those steep slopes and attempt to conquer them.

His pulse quickening, Cody joined the stream of personnel hurrying into the dining hall for a quick breakfast before assembling for the test.

Captain Westfall had informed his senior staff he wanted them at Test Control for the prebrief by 0730.

Jill came right from guard mount and arrived first. She'd reviewed the test plan with her personnel, deployed the necessary teams to the higher elevations and had Sergeant Barnes and another chase team standing by with their newly modified Humvees.

Excitement thrumming through her veins, she greeted the technicians manning the various monitoring stations. ''Mornin' team. Everyone ready for a good run?''

''We're ready.''

It sure looked like it from where Jill stood. Their racks of black boxes were lit up like Christmas trees, blinking red, glowing green, blipping gold dashes. The screens at each station displayed a similar rainbow of colors. If Pegasus so much as burped during his dash up the slopes, his handlers would know it instantly.

Kate showed up at Test Control a few minutes later. Unlike Jill, who wore her standard uniform of black beret, boots, BDUs, and her heavily laden bat belt with its assortment of police equipment, Kate was in khakis. Her flaming hair was neatly braided and tucked under a black ballcap that sported the red, white and blue Pegasus shield on its crown. She greeted Jill with a smile, excitement evident by the glint in her green eyes.

''Big day today.''

''Sure is.''

''If Pegasus jumps this hurdle, he'll only have one more land-based test before he gets to try his wings.''

Jill knew the schedule. The next—and final—land test included sending Pegasus galloping through clouds of simulated nuclear, chemical and biological hazards. Cody would switch from physician to nuclear-biological-chemical expert mode for that particular test.

And if Pegasus passed the final land test, Ditech would have lost out on any chance to get in on the multimillion-dollar project.

One more blow for Cody's former father-in-law. Jill had followed up on the tip passed to her by the research assistant at Decker Labs and checked out Jack Conway. If she'd read the financial reports right, Ditech had started a steep downward slide in recent years. Conway's attempt to profit from the recent antianthrax hysteria had only added to the slide, draining both funds and talent until Cody marshaled the board votes necessary to terminate the research. Jill had a feeling the doc wasn't on Conway's Christmas list anymore.

The door to the Control Center opened with a wrench.

"No, Major, I'm *not* prepared to alter the parameters for the first over-water test."

Her eyes stormy, Cari entered the center. Russ McIver followed hard on her heels. The marine's face was set in tight lines under the brim of his BDU field cap. He gave Kate and Jill a curt nod and sent his gaze back to the woman who was fast becoming his nemesis.

"If we maximize the load, we'll get a better read of how Pegasus handles with a full insertion team aboard."

"First we have to know how he handles *without* sixteen heavily armed Marines riding in his belly."

Jill wouldn't have thought Mac's jaw could torque any tighter. She was wrong.

"All I'm suggesting is that you increase the ballast by another five hundred pounds."

Cari drew herself up to her full height, which left her a good twelve inches short of the stiff-backed marine. "I'll discuss the matter with Captain Westfall."

"Do that, Lieutenant."

The two combatants retired to opposites sides of the Control Center, leaving Kate to arch a brow at Jill. Neither commented on the frosty relations between the Coast Guard and the Marine Corps, however, since the door opened once again to admit more of the senior staff. Cody arrived, as did Ed Santos, now fully recovered. The contractor's senior test pilot came next, followed by Captain Westfall and the Army officer who served as his exec.

The captain's glance skimmed the center, noting the staff members present. Everyone but the AF rep, Bill Thompson, had now assembled. Westfall's gaze cut to the large-display digital clock in the center bank of black boxes.

"We'll kick off the prebrief as soon as Colonel Thompson arrives. I suggest you fill your coffee mugs while we wait. Once we commence, there will be no breaks."

He made the suggestion in his normal voice, which

had all the resonance of a rusty bucket dropped down a deep well, but Jill could see he wasn't particularly pleased that his second-in-command was late.

She snagged a ceramic mug emblazoned with the cadre's shield and hit the coffeepot. Mug in hand, she moved to a niche between stands of black boxes. When Cody followed, Jill gave herself permission to imagine the play of his muscles under his crisply pressed khakis. For a moment. Only a moment.

"How did your computer search go?" she asked, sternly banishing the image of his naked chest and strong, corded thighs.

"It didn't. If our particular variation of the virus has struck anyone else, the Center for Disease Control has no record of it."

"That sounds like a plus to me. Maybe this little sucker is so rare and isolated it won't manifest itself again."

"Maybe."

Jill didn't want to stand in the way of medical research, but she sincerely hoped Ed Santos's bug had made its one and only appearance in this corner of the desert.

Her hopes took a nosedive not twenty minutes later, after a noticeably irritated Captain Westfall tried to contact Colonel Thompson via his eBook communicator. When Thompson didn't respond, Westfall turned to his staff.

"Anyone seen Colonel Thompson this morning?"

"I saw him when I came back from my run," Kate volunteered. "He was up and ready for the test but…"

"But what?"

"His face was flushed. I asked him if he was feeling okay. He said he was fine, just still a little heated from *his* morning workout."

Frowning, the captain sent his exec to Thompson's quarters. The young Army officer reported back within minutes.

"He's not in quarters. The door was unlocked, so I went inside and conducted a search."

Westfall whipped around to Jill. She already had her communicator off her belt.

"I'm on it, sir." Keying the transmit button, she raised Rattler Control. "I need a location for Colonel Bill Thompson. ASAP."

An uneasy silence gripped the senior staff members until the MP desk responded.

"We've got him, Rattler One. He's here on-site, just twenty or so meters from where you're standing. Looks like he's stationary. Want us to send someone to make contact?"

"I'll do it."

She found the colonel behind one of the modular units, lying facedown in the dirt.

Chapter 11

Jill dropped to her knees beside the Air Force officer. She didn't touch him, unsure at this point what had brought him down.

"Bill?"

When he made no response, she took his arm and gently rolled him over. The blue tinge to his lips stopped the breath in her lungs.

"Oh, no!"

She pressed two fingers to the side of his throat. No pulse. Her chest tight, she keyed her communicator.

"Control, this is Rattler One. We have what looks like a S-77. Advise Doc Richardson I'm starting CPR and get him here, fast!"

Waiting only for Rattler Control to acknowledge the coded signal indicating possible cardiac arrest, Jill threw the communications device aside. Her hands shook as she turned Bill's head to one side to clean his mouth of any obstructing matter. Repositioning him with his head back and his chin up, she pinched his nose, drew in a deep breath and closed her mouth over his. She blew in once, twice.

Again she felt for a pulse.

Still none.

Her heart pounding, she rose up on her knees and found the notch at the base of his breastbone. She stacked her hands above the notch, one on top of the other, locked her fingers, and pressed down.

"Fifteen-one, fifteen-two, fifteen-three…"

She was sweating by the time she counted out the fifteen compressions. Panting, she pinched Bill's nose again and stooped to breathe into him.

Once. Twice.

"Come on," she pleaded, stacking her hands once more. "You've got a wife and two kids. Come on, dammit!"

She was on her third set of compressions when she heard the thud of running footsteps. Cody rounded the back of the building, one of his hospital corpsman hard on his heels.

"We'll take him, Major. Move aside."

Sagging with relief, Jill yielded her place. Cody

dropped down beside the colonel and swiftly took his vitals.

"No blood pressure, no pulse, no respirations. We'll need the AED."

"Yes, sir."

Jill stood clear while the medic flipped open the lid on the AED—the Automated Emergency Defibrillator. Small, portable kits like this one were now carried on most commercial aircraft as well as being readily available in airports, schools, gambling casinos, and major sports facilities. Jill had purchased several of the inexpensive units for her detachment on the off chance one of the patrols working a remote section of the site might run into trouble. She'd also made sure her people had been trained in its operation.

This was the first time, though, she'd seen one put to use in anything other than a classroom situation. Her fists clenched at her sides, she watched Cody yank down the zipper on the colonel's flight suit and drag up his undershirt. A quick peel pulled the backing from the adhesive electrodes. Once they were affixed to Bill's chest, the AED's computer interpreted his heart rhythm and returned an almost instantaneous, metallic-sounding response.

"Press shock button."

Cody pushed the blinking red button. The jolt arched Bill's back and brought him off the ground. Thankfully, it also jump-started his heart.

"We've got a pulse. Let's intubate."

Jill murmured a silent prayer of thanks. Slumping against the wall of the modular unit, she watched while Cody worked a plastic tube down the colonel's throat. As soon as it was in place, the corpsman attached a tube with a dangling bag. The other end of the tube was connected to a small, portable oxygen bottle.

Relief sliced into Jill like a blade when the bag began to slowly inflate, then deflate.

Almost as soon as Cody had the colonel stabilized, he ordered an air evacuation to the Cardiac Care Unit at Kirtland. While his corpsmen loaded the patient aboard the helo, he instructed Jill to rinse her mouth thoroughly with antiseptic, then briefed Captain Westfall. The naval officer stood beside Cody at the helo pad, his face carved in granite as the doc pitched his voice to be heard over the whine of the chopper's engines warming up.

"Bill had an irregular heartbeat. Nothing major, and nothing that required medication. Under normal circumstances, it wouldn't have caused him any trouble. But preliminary indications are his temperature spiked so high it caused a severe arrhythmia, which in turn led to the heart attack. We won't know how much damage was done to the heart muscle until we get him into CCU."

''Do you think this sudden high fever was caused by the same bug that hit Ed Santos?''

''That's my guess.''

The captain's jaw tightened. ''Bill hasn't left the compound since he arrived. That means he picked up the virus here on-site.''

Cody had reached the same conclusion within seconds of arriving at the scene. ''I've told my folks to check the water containers again and do a thorough sweep of the dining hall. We've got to identify the source of the contamination. In the meantime, we'd better be prepared for the virus to infect more of our folks.''

Westfall nodded, his expression grim.

Cody glanced at the chopper, saw the pilot give a thumbs-up, ready-to-go signal. ''I'll get back to base as soon as I can.''

He stayed with Bill Thompson until the Air Force officer was coherent enough to understood his condition. Not only would he be unfit to return to duty anytime soon, it was doubtful he'd ever climb back into a cockpit. Glum but thankful to be alive, Thompson didn't recall being bitten by any ticks or mosquitoes, nor did Cody find any evidence of insect bites on his body. He did, however, admit to feeling dizzy during his workout at the gym that morning.

''Why didn't you report to the dispensary?'' Cody wanted to know.

"I was going to, but the dizziness let up," the macho pilot admitted sheepishly. "When it hit again, it came on so hard and fast, I just folded."

Cody was in the air and en route back to the Pegasus site a little past 3:00 p.m. Midway through the flight, he received word that another member of the test cadre was at the clinic, complaining of a headache and dizziness.

"It's one of my troops," Jill informed him when she met him at the helo pad. "Private First Class Harris."

Clamping her hand over her beret to keep it from being blown away by the still-rotating blades, she lengthened her stride to match Cody's.

"He was up in the mountains with one of the chase teams. I deployed two, well before the scheduled test run. Harris started feeling whoozy about an hour after he got in place but tried to tough it out."

Like Bill Thompson.

"We'll have to advise the rest of the test cadre not to play chicken with this virus," Cody said tersely. "It's too potent and too fast acting."

"Captain Westfall scrubbed today's test run," Jill informed him.

"I heard." Frowning, Cody started up the steps to the clinic. "A wise decision under the circumstances."

"Doc!"

He paused on the top step. "Yes?"

Concern darkened Jill's eyes to a deep coffee brown. "Harris is a good man. I'd hate to lose him."

"You won't," he stated with more confidence than he felt at the moment. He forced himself to relax his taut muscles and gave her a belated pat on the back. "You did great this morning, by the way. Really great."

"Thanks."

"Bill said to tell you he'll deliver a dozen roses and a big, fat kiss as soon as he's back on his feet."

"Well, that gives me something to look forward to."

"With any luck, I'll deliver before Bill does."

The drawled promise stayed with Jill long after she returned to Rattler Control. At guard mount later that evening, she briefed her people on the status of both Colonel Thompson and Private Harris.

"Don't try to macho this thing out," she added, mindful of Cody's advice. "If you start feeling dizzy or nauseous or achy, let someone know and report to the clinic immediately if you're able. If not, we'll come get you."

As she did most evenings, Jill drove her souped-up four-wheeler out into the desert to do a perimeter run and spot-check her patrols. The night was still and calm and so decked with stars it was hard to believe she'd fought desperately for a man's life only this morning.

"That was a close one, Goof."

The plastic toy Velcro'ed to the dash of her vehicle bobbed its head in acknowledgment.

"Too close," she murmured, only now allowing herself to feel the aftershocks. She slowed the ATV and waited for the tremors to subside.

It was close to midnight when she stopped by the clinic. The latest word from Albuquerque was that Bill Thompson was holding his own against the virus that had aggravated his heart murmur and sent him into cardiac arrest. So, thankfully, was Private Harris. Jill found the MP asleep in a cocoon of strategically placed cooling packs. An IV dripped a glucose solution into his veins to replace the liquids he'd lost to uncontrollable sweats.

Cody joined her a few moments later.

"Isn't there anything else we can do for Harris?" she asked.

"Our primary objective is to break the fever. Once he gets past that, recovery should be quick."

If he got past the raging fever, Cody thought. The damned virus was one of the more virulent he'd come up against in a long time. Frustration at his inability to cut the critter off at the source was starting to eat into him.

Hooking his hands on his stethoscope, he shifted his gaze from the restless MP to his commander. Worry for her subordinate had etched deep grooves in Jill's forehead. Fatigue had painted purple smudges under her eyes.

"How about you?" he asked. "How are you feeling?"

"Me? I'm fine. A little tired maybe, but no headaches, no achy muscles or bones."

"You look like hell."

She looked up, both startled and amused. "Is that a personal or a professional opinion?"

"Both."

Taking her elbow, he steered her out of the small ward area. The corpsman on duty that night gave them a nod as they passed.

"I know the kind of hours you've been putting in," Cody said firmly. "I also know how much the incident with Bill Thompson must have taken out of you. I'm prescribing six solid hours of sack time."

"Six hours. I wish! Captain Westfall has rescheduled the run for the day after tomorrow. He's also changed the test track. I'm going up into the mountains tomorrow to scan the area."

"You've got to slow down, woman. You're running on pure adrenaline."

"Like you're not?"

Holding open the door, he followed her outside. Their boots rang hollowly on the three metal steps leading down to the hard-packed dirt walkway.

Her ATV was parked a few yards away. Cody escorted her to the vehicle with every intention of sending her immediately to her quarters and to bed. The quiet of the night and the realization that it had been at least eighteen hours since he'd kissed this woman sabotaged those good intentions.

"Hey," he said as she slid into the driver's seat.

"What?"

Propping an elbow on the roll bar, he leaned down and brushed his knuckles along the warm skin of her throat. "I told you I'd deliver before Bill Thompson did."

"Here? Now?"

"You know how it is with those of us in the uniformed services," he murmured as his lips grazed hers. "Sometimes we have to take a target of opportunity."

He kept the kiss light, easy, more companionship than passion, since that was pretty well beyond him at this point. He was dead on his feet after a killer couple of days and a trip to the CCU he didn't want to repeat anytime soon. Yet something shifted inside him at the feel of Jill's mouth soft and warm and pliant under his.

It wasn't love. It couldn't be love. He'd only known the woman for a few weeks. Whatever it was, though, came pretty damn close. Shaken by the intensity of the feeling, Cody drew back a little and spotted the plastic toy on her dash.

"Who's that?"

"My pal." Jill gave the figure a flick with one

finger. He bobbed and grinned back at her. "Goofy goes with me everywhere. He's seen action in Korea, Colombia, Bosnia and half the fifty states."

"How did you two get so close?"

She caught her lower lip between her teeth. Cody saw the reluctance that flickered across her face, heard it in the small silence that spun out between them.

"Sorry. Didn't mean to intrude," he lied.

Nothing said she had to open up to him. He felt a gnawing need to connect on more than a physical level, but obviously she didn't. Easing his elbow from the roll bar, he was prepared to go back into the clinic when she broke the silence.

"Remember the jock I told you about? The one I tangled with in college?"

How could he forget? His glance went to the hair curving just above her collar. The smooth cap gleamed like summer wheat lit by a harvest moon and hid the ugly scar underneath.

"I remember," he said grimly.

"He was too big for me, too strong. After that incident, I was determined no goon would get the best of me again."

"So you took self-defense courses and, ultimately, became a cop."

"Correct. I also convinced myself muscles were a serious turnoff. Ever since that incident, I've dated only gangly, awkward types. Like Goofy."

Cody didn't rank anywhere near Arnold Schwarzenegger when it came to physique, but genetics had presented him with a big frame and a solid build. Jill must have forced herself to overcome an aversion that had been seared into her psyche when she took him into her arms and into her body. The realization hit him with almost as much force as the suspicion that he'd fallen for this woman.

Hard.

"You should have told me," he growled. "I would have taken things slower in Albuquerque. Given you more time to adjust to my size and weight."

Jill tipped her head. He'd just handed her the perfect excuse to pull back, to retreat behind the old, familiar walls. All the reasons why she should do just that raced through her mind.

"I didn't want to take things slower," she said, her gaze clear and direct. "I was every bit as hungry as you were."

Nothing had changed. They both still had important jobs to do. The mission came first. It had to come first. Yet she couldn't deny how she felt any longer.

"I'm still hungry," she admitted gruffly.

"Now she tells me!"

His theatrical groan dragged a grin from Jill. Her hands came up, grasped the lapel of his lab coat, hauled him back down until their breath mingled.

"I've changed my mind, big guy. Or rather you changed it. I like the way we fit together."

"So do I," he growled.

Cody's bone-deep weariness evaporated. Suddenly companionship was the last thing on his mind. He covered her mouth with his, and there was nothing slow or easy or comfortable about this kiss.

She hadn't lied about her hunger. It arced between them. He welcomed the heat of it, the hard, swift punch. His belly clenching, he buried his hands in her hair and tipped her head back.

His lab coat bunched in her fists. Her mouth fused with his. She held nothing back. Nothing. Cody was within a heartbeat of dragging her out of the ATV when he realized there was no place to drag her *to*.

Certainly not back into the clinic. Professional ethics and one very sick patient nixed that idea. Nor could they retreat to their quarters. She shared the larger unit with Cari and Kate. Cody and Russ McIver bunked down in one of the smaller units.

It was a measure of how desperately he wanted this woman that he actually considered flipping down the rear seat of the Lincoln. The monumentally stupid idea wrung a groan from him. A genuine one this time.

"If we don't stop now," he said, his heart slamming against his ribs, "Goofy here is going to get an eyeful."

"Think so?"

"I do." He dropped another fierce kiss on her lips and released her. "Go back to your quarters. Hit the rack. Get some sleep."

"Oh, yeah. As if either of us will be able to shut down our systems now."

She released his lapels and smoothed the wrinkled white cotton. Her palms slid down his chest, bumped over his uniform belt, dipped lower. Cody sucked in a swift breath and jerked away from the vehicle.

"Go!"

"Okay, okay. I'm out of here."

Keying the ignition, Jill put the ATV in drive. She took a last look at Cody in the rearview mirror and felt her whole body shudder with need.

"Oooh, boy, Goof. I've got it bad. Real bad."

Her buddy bobbed his head in vigorous agreement.

Chapter 12

To Jill's surprise, she welcomed the glow of lamplight behind the blinds of the modular unit she shared with Kate and Caroline. Cody's kiss had pushed her bone-deep weariness to the back burner and left her much too keyed up to sleep. She needed to decompress.

She parked the ATV outside the unit, thinking how much her perspective had changed in the past few weeks. The stolen hours in Cody's arms had pretty well demolished her self-imposed aversion to muscled, athletic men. Kate's irrepressible good nature and Cari's quiet friendship had done the same to her doubts about sharing a cramped set of quarters with two other women.

Her roommates were engaged in their usual after-hours pursuits, she saw when she stepped inside. The petite Coast Guard officer was curled up in the unit's one comfortable chair with a thriller. Kate was on a laptop computer, playing some crazy atmospheric ionization game with a group of space nuts she'd stumbled across on the Internet. The encrypted computer shielded her identity and location, but nothing could suppress her expertise. Most nights she whacked the other players.

''There you are,'' the vivacious redhead said. ''We were about to send out the search-and-rescue team. How's Private Harris?''

''Still feverish but holding his own.''

''Good.'' Kate cocked her head and studied Jill's face. ''Either you've taken to wearing blush on your chin or you've got a nice little whisker burn going there. Wish the doc gave that kind of personal attention to all his patients.''

''I'm sure Private Harris would appreciate it,'' Jill retorted with a grin as she tossed her hat on the table. Unbuckling her bat belt, she wrapped the thick leather with all its accoutrements around the holstered Beretta, laid the bundle beside her hat and sank into the chair next to Cari's. Every bone in her body sighed in relief.

''Lord, what a day.''

''Any late word on Bill Thompson?''

''Cody checked with the CCU while I was at the

clinic. Bill's stable, but it's not looking good that he'll ever climb back into a cockpit. Depending on the amount of damage to his heart, he may be facing a medical retirement.''

"That sucks,'' Kate said succinctly.

"Big-time,'' Cari added, propping her paperback on her bent knee. "I couldn't imagine not pulling on a uniform every morning.''

"Neither can I,'' Jill agreed, "but we'll all have to hang it up sometime.''

She tipped Cari a curious glance. Although the Coast Guard officer's slight stature and slender curves gave her a youthful air, she had more time in uniform than either Jill or Kate.

"You're past the halfway mark to retirement. Are you going to go the stretch?''

"That's the plan.''

"What about that Navy JAG back in Washington?'' Kate asked. "The one who's had calls forwarded to you at least six times since we've been on-site, not that anyone's counting. Is he in for the duration, too?''

"He is. He's almost as gung-ho as our resident leatherneck.''

Kate snorted. "*No* one can be as gung-ho as Russ McIver.''

"Trust me, Jerry comes close." Sighing, the brunette riffled the pages of her book. "He thinks it's great we both have careers and share similar experiences. So do I, except I want to make room in my life for children, too.''

''And Jerry doesn't?''

''He's got three kids by his ex-wife. He knows firsthand how difficult it is to raise a family while one parent pulls sea duty. He thinks two parents at sea would stack the odds against us.''

''He's got a point there.'' Kate clicked off her computer and pulled down the lid. Her green eyes held a rueful sympathy. ''I've been down that road. My ex and I didn't have kids, but we had everything else working against us. Weird hours, long separations, one of us on a faster career track than the other. It takes more determination than either of us apparently possessed to make that kind of marriage work.''

''Maybe you just didn't try it with the right guy,'' Cari said gently.

''Obviously.'' Stretching like a cat, Kate bent her arms and hooked them behind her neck. ''What about you, Jillium? How do you envision things working out between you and our hunky doc? Or haven't you reached the talking-about-the-relationship stage yet?''

Jill had given up trying to deflect Kate's natural inquisitiveness. After weeks of living almost in each other's pockets, she had few secrets left from either of these women.

"We're not anywhere near the talking-about-things stage."

Even Cari laughed at that one. "You may not be, but it sure looks to me like Cody's fast approaching the go, no-go point. You'd better start thinking about a game plan for when we wrap up this project and you two go your separate ways."

"Speaking of wrapping up this project," Jill said, neatly turning the discussion, "the Air Force will have to identify a replacement for Bill Thompson pretty fast or the schedule will take another serious hit."

"Captain Westfall's already approved Bill's replacement," Kate informed them. "He told me at supper," she added when both women turned to stare at her.

"Who is it?"

"Some jet jockey by the name of Dave Scott."

"What's the skinny on him?"

"I know nothing...yet."

"But you will," Jill said, grinning. "By the time the poor man reports on-site, you'll have scoped out everything down to and including his shoe size."

"Scott's going to have it tough," Cari observed. "We've got the advantage of having worked together for several weeks now. He'll have to hump to make up for lost time."

"Hopefully he'll fit in as well as Bill did," Jill said, although the prospect of factoring a new, unknown personality into the small test cadre didn't appeal to her any more than it did to the others. Their group had jelled into a tight-knit team. A stranger would upset the balance they'd worked out over the past weeks.

Well, they'd face that problem—if it was one— when Dave Scott arrived. Right now Jill had enough real concerns on her plate without worrying about potential ones.

A jaw-cracking yawn told her the high from those moments with Cody outside the clinic had fizzled. She was completely and totally decompressed. Dragging herself out of her chair, she gathered her gear.

"I've got to get some sleep. Doctor's orders."

Cari uncurled and rose, as well. "I hope you get through the night without a call."

"So do I!"

Jill almost made it.

The direct-line phone beside her bed jangled less than a half hour before the time she'd set on her digital alarm. Grimacing at the glowing green digits, she fumbled for the phone.

"Bradshaw."

"This is Rattler Control. Sorry to wake you, ma'am."

"No problem." She struggled upright and hooked her tangled hair behind her ears. "What's up?"

"We just got a call routed through the central switchboard from a Jack Conway."

She tried to shake off the cobwebs. "Who's Jack Conway?"

"He says he's the president and CEO of some company called Ditech."

That snapped Jill out of her grogginess. Conway, she belatedly recalled, was also the father of Cody's dead wife.

"What does he want?"

"He's trying to track down Doc Richardson. Say's the doc hasn't returned his phone calls and he's worried about him. Sounded more pissed than worried, if you ask me."

"Did you advise Dr. Richardson of the call?"

"No, ma'am. Since Conway's not on the doc's immediate access list, I told the man I'd pass the message. That really set him off." The controller hesitated a moment. "At that point he started making what sounded a whole lot like threats to me, ma'am."

"Threats?" Hooking her legs over the edge of the mattress, Jill sat up. "I'll take the call. Patch him through on a secure line."

"Yes, ma'am."

While her on-duty controller made the patch, she squinted at the clock again. Five-twenty New Mexico time. Just past seven on the East Coast, assuming that's where Conway was located.

''Good ahead, ma'am.''

''Good morning, Mr. Conway. I understand you're trying to reach…''

''Who the hell is this?''

''Major Jill Bradshaw, United States Army. I'm responding to your call to Dr. Cody Richardson.''

''Why are you responding? Where is that bastard?''

Whoa! No wonder Cody hadn't added this guy to his immediate access list.

''Dr. Richardson is working a special project for the government at an undisclosed location. I'm responding because your call was routed through…''

''I want to talk to him. Now!''

''…our switchboard,'' Jill finished firmly. ''If you'll tell me why you need to contact Dr. Richardson, I'll relay the message.''

''Listen, little girl, I don't discuss family business with anyone who isn't family. You get my son-in-law on the line and you get him fast.''

''Family business? Does this concern Ditech?''

''You're damned right it concerns Ditech.''

''It's my understanding Dr. Richardson put his holdings in that company in a blind trust.''

There was a short, heavy silence.

''*Who* is this?'' Conway asked again.

''Major Jill Bradshaw.''

''How do you know about Cody's holdings?''

"I had occasion to review his financial disclosure statement," she replied with purposeful vagueness.

There was another silence while Conway digested that bit of information.

"Then you know he retained his seat on my company's board of directors," he said after a moment.

"Yes, I do."

"And you probably also know the company is facing bankruptcy."

She returned a noncommittal answer, although her own research into the company and the artless disclosures of the young research assistant at Decker Labs had pretty well confirmed that Ditech was in dire financial straits.

It soon became apparent Jack Conway didn't share the young assistant's assertion that Cody had single-handedly kept the company alive and breathing. Bitterness eating like acid through his voice, the man ignored his just-stated prohibition against discussing family business outside the family.

"You tell that bastard I want his proxy vote on the new stock issue today. He killed my daughter. I'll be damned if I'll let him kill my company, too."

Jill shot upright on the edge of the mattress. "What did you say?"

"You heard me."

"Mr. Conway, are you alleging Dr. Richardson caused his wife's death?"

The hatred spewed through the phone like hot,

scorching lava. "I'm not alleging anything. I'm telling you straight-out. Cody Richardson killed her. My baby. My Alicia."

Jill's knuckles went white on the receiver. Stunned, she could only listen as Conway snarled into her ear.

"You tell Richardson I'd better get his vote. Today!"

"I'll tell him."

"If Ditech goes down, I'll make damned sure he goes with it. You can tell him that, too."

If she hadn't been struggling to absorb what she'd just heard, Jill might have winced at the crash of the receiver slamming down. The clatter barely registered on her consciousness.

She forced her mind to cut through the kaleidoscope of her whirling thoughts and buzzed Rattler Control again.

"What's Doc Richardson's present location?"

With a few clicks of the keys, the controller pulled up the signal for the locator embedded in Cody's holographic ID.

"I make him still at the clinic. Must have slept there."

Jill swallowed the lump that kept trying to form in her dry throat. "Get on the horn to the Virginia Highway Patrol. Ask them to fax the report of the vehicle accident in which Dr. Richardson's wife was killed. It happened about three years ago. Her name was Alicia. Alicia Conway Richardson.''

"Will do.''

"I'll swing by and pick up the report in a few minutes.''

"Roger.''

Grimly Jill threw back the sheet and headed for the bathroom. When she arrived at the MP headquarters, she received the accident report from Rattler Control and a report from the glum Sergeant Barnes that the squadron mascot had died during the night.

"Guess he didn't take to captivity.''

"Guess not,'' Jill muttered, skimming the report. She had other things on her mind right now besides a scaly diamondback. Foremost amongst them was the accident that killed Cody Richardson's wife.

Cody hadn't slept all night.

His eyes burned with fatigue, and every muscle in his body cried to go horizontal, but an after-midnight arrival at the clinic had put all thought of bed out of his mind.

The Pegasus virus had struck again. One of the cooks from the dining hall had staggered in complaining of dizziness, stomach cramps and nausea. He was also burning with fever. Like Colonel Thompson and Private Harris, the man hadn't been off-site since his arrival.

Cody started him on Ibuprofen and took turns with the corpsman on duty wiping both him and Harris down with cool cloths. With its limited staff, his small clinic wouldn't be able to handle many more patients.

Nor could he put off reporting these cases to the Center for Disease Control any longer. Dr. Nez and the folks at Decker had notified CDC of the serology of the new strain. It was time to fill them in on its activity to date.

Cody had already cleared the call with Captain Westfall. He'd also precoordinated with the CDC to determine who had the necessary security clearances to protect the information he intended to relay. It was still early, he noted with a quick glance at his watch, not quite eight o'clock East Coast time, but the individual he needed to talk to should be in by now.

He was in his office, about to request a secure line from the Control Center, when Jill appeared. For the first time since the pale, sweating cook had staggered into the clinic, Cody relaxed and allowed himself the simple pleasure of a smile.

"'Morning."

"Are you busy?"

"Another one of the cadre came down sick last night. I was just about to notify the Center for Disease Control of our problem."

A flicker crossed her face, as if that was just one more worry added to her pile, but she didn't comment on the fact that maintaining the security of the Pegasus site might soon get a whole lot more difficult.

"I need to talk to you."

"What about?"

"About the phone call I just intercepted from a Mr. Jack Conway."

Well, hell! That's all Cody needed right now.

The familiar mix of guilt and regret clutched at his insides. Part of him marveled that he hadn't felt those twin claws digging into him for some time now. Other, more pressing matters had blunted the sharp talons. Like the Pegasus project. And the woman standing just inside his office.

Tipping back in his chair, Cody eyed her stiff spine and squared shoulders. It was obvious Conway had given her an earful.

"Let me guess," he drawled. "Jack's pissed because I haven't responded to the dozen or so blistering messages he's left on my answering machine at home. Just out of curiosity, how did he reach you?"

"Evidently he called your supervisor at the National Institute for Health, who told him you were working a special project. Your boss routed the call to the Department of Defense, who…"

"Routed it here," Cody finished. "Sorry the old man flushed you out of bed. He can be a real bastard when he wants to."

"As a matter of fact, Mr. Conway said the same thing about you."

His mouth twisted. "That doesn't surprise me."

"He said to tell you he wants your proxy vote on a new stock issue today."

She delivered the message very deliberately, each word measured and precise. Cody could guess the vitriol that had come with it.

He brought his chair tipping forward with a thump. Frustration surged through him in hot, angry spikes. Damn Jack, anyway! His daughter's death had left him so angry and bitter he'd destroy Ditech just to get back at the son-in-law he once trusted to run his company. Cody had hoped the anger would ease with time. Instead, it had eaten into the man's soul. Now Conway had dragged Jill into the morass of his hatred and enmity.

"I've already told Jack twice I won't support his plan to spin off one of Ditech's divisions and put out an IPO," he said evenly. "That's an Initial Public Offering of stock, designed to bring in—"

"I know what an IPO is."

Cody narrowed his eyes at the clipped response. Belatedly he realized she'd switched into full cop mode. He kicked himself for not noticing it before this point. He could only blame his bone-deep weariness.

"I'm a little slow on the uptake here," he said, his gaze locked with hers. "I should have realized you tracked me down to do more than deliver a message about the stock issue.''

''Why else would I track you down?''

''You tell me.''

''All right.''

She didn't pull her punches. Her voice hard and flat, she put the issue squarely between them.

''Your father-in-law said you killed your wife. Care to tell me why he'd make such an allegation?''

Cody's jaw clenched. He'd expected the accusation. Had heard it countless times before. Skewered by his guilt, he gave her the only answer he could.

''Because it's true.''

Chapter 13

Jill wasn't buying Cody's confession. She'd pored over every detail of the incident report the Virginia Highway Patrol had faxed in. The report documented a rain-drenched night. A high-powered Mercedes convertible driven much too fast for the slick roads. A turn taken too sharply. The investigating officers hadn't so much as hinted the deadly crash was anything other than an accident.

Yet Jack Conway certainly believed otherwise. And Cody had just flat-out stated his culpability.

"When a man voluntarily admits to killing his wife," she said, still struggling to make sense of this, "the appropriate response at that point is to Mirandize him."

"Before he incriminates himself any further?" His mouth took a bitter twist. "You don't have to read me my rights. I'm guilty as hell, but not in the eyes of the law."

"Then maybe we'd better back up a step here. What happened to your wife?"

"Exactly what I told you the last time you asked me. She died in a car crash. What I didn't tell you is what led up to the accident." His eyes went bleak. "And what came after."

"I'm listening."

"Not here," he said grimly, pushing out of his chair. "Let me check on my patients and I'll meet you outside."

That worked for Jill. She needed to get past the aftershocks, to let the predawn air clear her head.

She went outside and leaned against the fender of her ATV. She'd driven the ATV the short distance to the clinic with the fuzzy thought that she'd drive up into the mountains as planned after talking to Cody. Now she could barely remember climbing into the vehicle, much less crossing the compound. His stark admission of guilt had driven everything else out of her head.

Cody pushed through the door of the clinic a few moments later. The cords in his neck were as tight as steel cables. His shoulders had knotted under his lab coat. He saw Jill take off her cap and shag an unsteady hand through her hair, and the irony bit into his soul.

He'd kissed her here, in this exact same spot, only a few hours ago. He'd brushed a hand down her cheek and felt the ground tilt a few degrees.

Now...

Now she squared her hat back on her head and regarded him with the cool, assessing gaze of a cop.

"Alicia and I argued the night she died," he began without preamble. "It wasn't the first time by any means, but we both said some things that night that didn't need saying. She was crying when she snatched up her car keys and ran out of the house."

The shouts and recriminations from her rang in Cody's head. He didn't love her. He'd never loved her. He'd only married her because of the fat research budget her father had dangled in front of him. He'd used Ditech to build his reputation, and if he thought he was going to walk away from their marriage with fifty percent of the stock he'd acquired over the years, he had another think coming.

She'd refused to believe he didn't want the damned stock, that he didn't want the eight-thousand-square-foot town house in Maclean, didn't want to stay locked in a marriage that had hit bottom years ago. Nor did he have any desire to continue working for a company where research was channeled more by potential profit than by science, but Alicia had refused to believe that, too.

A rain-slick street had forever silenced their bitter arguing, and guilt still corroded Cody's conscience.

"It was raining." He forced each word, reliving the nightmare that came with them. "Alicia lost control of her car and slammed into a bridge abutment. Since she'd run out without her purse or any form of ID, I didn't learn about the accident until the Highway Patrol traced the vehicle's registration."

"Through Ditech."

"Through Ditech. By the time I got to the hospital, Alicia had suffered massive cerebral hemorrhaging and had been declared brain dead. I signed the consent form to harvest her organs and take her off the respirator later that afternoon."

Jill sucked in a swift breath. Cody heard the small hiss, registered the sympathy buried in the small sound, rejected it. He didn't want pity from her. Or anyone else.

"Jack Conway has never forgiven me for signing the consent form," he stated flatly. "He never will."

"And you've never forgiven yourself?"

He made a quick, impatient gesture of denial. "I examined Alicia and concurred in the diagnosis of brain death. I don't regret taking her off life support and harvesting her organs. As a doctor, I *can't* regret that."

"All right. As a husband, then. You blame yourself for the argument that sent your wife running out of the house in tears?"

"I'll always carry the blame for that."

The flat statement lifted some of the weight from Jill's chest. Cody's next words piled it right on again.

"Alicia was Jack's only child. It didn't take long for his pain at losing her to spill over into hate. He's convinced I retained my seat on Ditech's board because I'm out to destroy the company, just like I destroyed his daughter."

"That's pretty much what he said."

"He doesn't care that I risked my standing with the Public Health Service by asking to be excluded from any research involving Ditech. Or that I sank every penny I had into the company to keep it afloat after one of his more disastrous decisions."

"The flawed research for an antianthrax vaccine?"

"You know about that?"

"Rob, the young research assistant at Decker, said you forced Conway to terminate the project."

"I did."

"Which gave him one more reason to hate you."

Something nibbled at the edge of Jill's mind, something that wouldn't quite come into focus. Frowning, she tried to recall Conway's exact words.

"Your father-in-law said you would both go down if the company failed."

Cody's shoulders lifted under the white lab coat. "That's true enough. I put my Ditech stock in a blind trust. I couldn't dump it if I wanted to. After the anthrax fiasco, I used my other stocks and bonds as collateral for a loan to make payroll and operating expenses.''

''So Jack Conway not only hates you,'' Jill said slowly, ''he owes you. That's a pretty potent combination.''

''I know.'' The stiffness went out of Cody's shoulders. Pity stirred in his face. ''I also understand how hard the past three years have been on him.''

Jill didn't feel quite the sympathy for Conway that he obviously did, but then she hadn't lived through the hell the two men had.

''Those years have been hard on you, too, Cody. Isn't it time you cut yourself a little slack?''

He blew out a long breath and looked to the gold and red dawn spearing up from behind the jagged peaks of the Guadalupes. When he brought his glance back to Jill, it lingered on her face.

''Maybe it is.''

His tension might have eased a little, but she was still wound tight. She scrubbed a hand over the back of her neck, kneading the knots. She needed to think. She also needed more information on a certain Jack Conway.

''Look, I've got to make a run up into the mountains to preview the track Pegasus will take tomorrow. Can we talk more about your father-in-law when I get back?''

''We've pretty well covered all the bases.''

Maybe. Maybe not. Jill couldn't shake the feeling

she'd missed something, either in her conversation with Cody or in the call from Conway.

"I'll see you then."

Preoccupied with her thoughts, she slid into the driver's seat and missed seeing the step Cody took toward her. About to reach meltdown point, he decided to take another quick check on his patients and hit the shower before making the call to his contact at the CDC.

Jill mulled over everything Cody had told her during the drive up the mountains. They loomed ahead, rising out of the scorching desert floor like the backbone of some monstrous dinosaur. The bare granite peaks glistened in the sun, but the scattered stands of juniper and ponderosa pine dotting the slopes gave some promise of shade. The end of August was fast approaching, but the sun hadn't lost its brutal daytime punch. Sweat trickled between Jill's breasts and stuck her brown T-shirt to her back. Her lightweight BDUs felt as heavy and hot as canvas.

"Guess we should have ridden in the Humvee instead of taking this ATV," she muttered to Goofy as they jounced along the ruts that passed for a road. "At least the Hummer's enclosed and air-conditioned."

A glance in the rearview mirror showed the chase vehicle lumbering along behind. With the recently installed mods, the tanklike Humvee had no difficulty keeping up with Jill's lighter, faster ATV. Now the question was whether the heavily armed chase vehicles could keep up with Pegasus when he charged up the mountains tomorrow.

"Assuming he gets to slip his halter," Jill muttered to her traveling companion. "If this damned bug infects any more of our little band of warriors, we can forget about putting Pegasus through his paces for a while."

The prospect of additional delays added to the nervous tension rolling around in her stomach. Things were heating up in the Middle East again. American troops were also slogging through jungles in Indonesia and the Philippines in search of terrorist training cells. The antidrug war in South and Central America had been shoved to the back burner since 9/11, but it still consumed incredible resources and personnel. Pegasus had been designed to operate in all these environments. He was desperately needed in the field.

Her hands slick with sweat, Jill gripped the wheel. Every bone-rattling jounce set her thoughts churning along with her stomach. Like a badminton shuttlecock, her mind batted back and forth between preplanning tomorrow's mission, the call from Jack Conway and the virus attacking personnel at the site.

"Why only us?" she asked Goofy. "Why no one else? And what's spawning the damned thing?"

The long-eared hound offered no answer to the puzzle.

"Then there's that business about desert sand storms and depleted uranium particles."

Jill had lost a few hours of sleep thinking about the Gulf War research Cody had mentioned.

"What if someone knew about that research?" she said, bouncing her thoughts off the plastic figure on the dash. "What if they wanted to test the theory that nasal irritation lessened a soldier's ability to block inhalation of harmful airborne particles? Maybe they wanted to develop—and sell to the Department of Defense—a nasal spray or a mask or a filter that purified the air?"

Like the ultraviolet water purifier Ditech had developed to aid earthquake-devastated Guatemala. Simple, inexpensive, easy to use, but now in such demand worldwide it had made the company billions.

Jill's stomach clenched. Another big win like that would certainly lift Ditech out of its present doldrums. Jack Conway wouldn't go down. Neither would his son-in-law, whose financial future was inextricably tied to that of the man's company.

No!

Her mind slammed the trapdoor on that thought before it could crawl out into the searing light of the desert. No way Cody would release a laboratory-altered bug at the site for any personal gain.

But Conway might. Assuming he somehow found out about the top-secret project Cody had been detailed to work.

Scowling at the stretch of sand still ahead, Jill shoved back her black felt beret and swiped her arm across her sweaty forehead.

"Maybe that call last night wasn't about voting a stock option," she said, still thinking out loud. "Maybe Conway just wanted to talk to Cody and try to find out what was happening at the site."

Like Cody, he'd have access to the Center for Disease Control's databases. Ditech was first and foremost a pharmaceutical company, after all, and the whole purpose of the database was to disseminate information about diseases. Conway could have searched for reports of an outbreak of an illness caused by a new strain of virus. He'd know it would have to be reported sooner or later for the public's safety. And he'd be all ready with a possible solution to the problem.

Only the CDC hadn't reported an outbreak. Right now no one knew how many folks had been infected except Cody.

And he intended to report it today.

"Dammit!"

She pounded a fist on the steering wheel. Everything kept coming back to Cody. The realization had her stomach pumping pure acid, but the cop in her wouldn't let go of the notion. Like a hunting dog worrying a rabbit, she chased it around and around in her mind until a call from the Humvee broke into her chaotic thoughts.

"Rattler One, this is Rattler Four."

"Go ahead, Four."

"We've been showing an engine-warning light for the past couple of miles. Looks like we'll have to return to base."

Jill mouthed a silent curse. Could anything else happen to delay tomorrow's run?

"Roger, Four. I'll continue up the proposed course and confirm the prepositioning coordinates. Advise me when you get back to the site and determine what the problem is."

"Will do."

Squinting through her sunglasses, Jill eyed the slopes ahead. The proposed course would take Pegasus up the rock-strewn lower elevations, through the conifer-dusted higher reaches, and across a trickling stream. The same stream, in fact, that pooled to form a convenient trysting spot for the skinny-dipping lovers her troops had stumbled upon a few days ago. Jill smiled grimly at the memory and aimed her ATV at a barely discernible track at the base of the lower slope.

"Hang on, Goof. This is going to be a rocky ride."

As the vehicle rattled and bumped up the slope, she clenched her teeth so tight an ache started in her jaw and lanced into her skull. Her head was pounding by the time she reached the first prepositioning point at the five-thousand-foot elevation mark.

She left the ATV idling while she climbed out to survey the location. The high elevation offered a panoramic view. Far below, the desert shimmered in the morning heat. Above, the achingly blue sky stretched for endless miles. All around her, the thin air carried the scent of pine and juniper.

The spot was perfect.

Although they had no reason to suspect overhead satellite surveillance, the screen of piñon would provide some cover for the Humvee. They were everywhere, those dark-needled pines. Their reddish bark gave off a pungent, cedarlike odor that wrinkled Jill's nose. She knew the piñon's seeds were the stuff of life in New Mexico. Animals feasted on their rich nutrients, and humans consumed them in everything from salads to thick, chewy caramel clusters.

Not just animals and humans, she saw when she turned to walk back to her vehicle. Reptiles, too, apparently.

Gulping, Jill stopped dead. The snake was almost lost in the shade of the piñon a few feet from the parked ATV. It was smaller than the Western diamondback that had sunk its fangs into Sergeant Barnes. One of the black-tailed rattlers they'd been told to watch out for on the slopes, especially at higher elevations.

This particular black-tail wasn't coiled to strike, she noted with heart-pounding relief. It lay stretched out in the dirt like a lazy gray S.

Step by cautious step, Jill backed away from the driver's side of her vehicle. By the time she'd scrambled in the passenger side and crawled over the console into to her seat, she was swimming in a nervous sweat. Sincerely hoping the snake hadn't decided to crawl in with her, she unsnapped the flap on her holster.

She wrapped her sweat-slick hand around the butt of her Beretta. Inch by cautious inch, she leaned out of the vehicle to check on the reptile. It was still there, stretched out under the piñon, unmoving. Only then did Jill notice the gnats swarming around its black, unblinking eyes. Her breath escaping on a wheeze, she flopped back against her seat.

"It's dead, Goof. My heart's about to break the world record for beats per minute and the thing's dead."

The incident left a chalky taste in her mouth. A quick swig from the water bottle she always carried as a precaution against the desert heat got rid of most of the dryness. Nevertheless, her hands shook when she put the vehicle in gear and aimed it up the slope again.

The altitude was starting to get to her, Jill decided when she and Goofy had bumped up an additional thousand feet. She was steering around a stand of fragrant juniper when another possibility worked its way through the fuzz in her head.

Maybe it wasn't the altitude causing these shakes. Maybe she'd caught the damned bug!

She certainly had the sweats. Her mouth was as dry as two-day-old toast. She'd blamed the ache in her skull on the bone-jarring ride, but she'd made the ride before and never experienced this steady, throbbing pain.

Grimly Jill angled the ATV onto a relatively level patch of dirt. Her head wasn't just pounding now, it was booming with all the sound and fury of an artillery barrage.

"We'd better get down this mountain and hightail it back to base, Goof."

She shoved the gearshift into reverse and backed the ATV up. Or tried to. The level patch was too narrow for a complete turn. Blinking the sweat out of her burning eyes, she pushed the gearshift into drive again. Her boot pressed the accelerator.

Too hard.

Too fast.

Jill's leg muscles had gone soft on her, as limp as wet paper. She struggled to lift her foot, missed the brake, hit the edge of the accelerator again. The ATV shot off the small ledge and went airborne.

It landed with a thud that almost cracked Jill's jaw. She fought the wheel, the brake, the steeply angled slope that seemed determined to tip the vehicle end over end.

A gnarled juniper clung to the rocks a little way to the left. Jill leaned on the wheel, sent the ATV straight at the tree. The spindly trunk bent almost to the ground, shuddered and held only long enough for Jill to throw herself out of the vehicle. She hit the ground and tumbled down the rocks in the ATV's crashing, careening wake.

Frantically she scrabbled for a hold. Any hold. The rocks she grabbed at tore right out of her hand. Scratchy weeds came loose at the roots.

She didn't see the jagged-edged finger of granite jutting out of the slope until the split second before she slammed into it.

Chapter 14

After a hot, soaking shower, Cody started for the clinic, intending to make his call to the Center for Disease Control. A growling stomach and the realization that he hadn't eaten in almost twenty-four hours had him detouring to the dining hall, where he spotted Kate Hargrave, Ed Santos, and Russ McIver.

"Hey, Doc."

Kate was wearing thigh-hugging black bicycle shorts and a sleeveless T-shirt over a sports bra. Still flushed from her morning run, the woman exuded a healthy—and very sensual—vitality. Cody appreciated the package. Any man with a half a drop of testosterone left in his body would. But his thoughts were on Kate's roommate as he joined the group.

Jill should be well up in the mountains by now. They'd have to talk when she got back and had time to sort through the ugly revelations about his marriage. He couldn't believe he'd laid all that on her. He could only attribute it to his weariness and the impetus of Jack Conway's call.

"Have a seat."

Kate waved him to a chair. McIver was more formal. Mindful of Cody's superior rank, the marine stood. "Good morning, Commander."

"'Morning, Mac."

"I hear you have another patient," Ed Santos commented. "How is he?"

"About as miserable as you were those first twenty-four hours."

The test engineer shuddered. "Poor kid."

"What's the latest on Colonel Thompson?" Kate asked.

"They're going to keep him in CCU until they determine the extent of the damage to his heart muscle. After that, he'll face a medical review board to determine his fitness to stay on active duty."

The confirmation that they'd lost one of their own cast a pall over the table. Hunching her sweat-sheened shoulders, Kate pushed her scrambled eggs around her plate with her fork.

"The Air Force has already identified a replacement for Bill," she told the group. "A fighter pilot by the name of Dave Scott."

Russ McIver's head whipped around. "Captain Dave Scott?"

"I think that's his rank. Why? Do you know him?"

"I know *of* him."

Kate stopped playing with her eggs. "Okay, McIver, give. Tell us what you know."

Mac opened his mouth, shut it again with a snap. To Kate's obvious disgust, all he would say was that Captain Scott had a reputation as one hell of a pilot in Special Operations circles. Excusing himself, the marine gathered his tray and left.

"No wonder the guy gets Cari's back up," Kate muttered. "He wouldn't bend if we hung a five-hundred-pound weight around his neck."

Cody kept silent. He'd had plenty of time to form his own opinion of both the stiff-necked marine and the petite, dark-haired Coast Guard officer. When it came to bending, he hadn't seen any evidence Cari Dunn would give all that easily, either.

As inevitably happened with any gathering of the test cadre, the conversation turned to the run scheduled for the following day. Again Cody kept silent. His pending call to the Center for Disease Control could well result in another delay. CDC might quarantine everyone on-site until the source of the mysterious virus was identified or the sudden outbreak of illness had run its course.

Frustrated all over again at his inability to find the

source, Cody finished his breakfast and made his way to the clinic. A call to the central switchboard got him a secure line and a patch through to Dr. John Long. The head of the CDC greeted him with one of his legendary foghorn bellows.

"Richardson! Why haven't I seen your ugly mug at staff meetings in the past few weeks?"

"I'm working a special project."

"That must be the reason my folks can't blast anything of NIH."

"I don't run the entire National Institute of Health," Cody reminded him mildly. "Only one department."

"Yeah, well, your department is usually the most cooperative, but I have to tell you we've been getting nothing but flack on that report about the global re-indicators of tuberculosis."

"I'll make a call. In return, I need a favor from you, John."

"You got it."

"Did you happen to see a notification of a new strain of flavivirus filed by Dr. Sylvia Nez?"

"Are you working with Sylvia? You lucky dog! That woman is every sex-starved research scientist's fantasy come to life. Brilliant *and* hot!"

"The report, John. Did you see it?"

"I saw it. Another addition to the bad bug book. We seem to be getting a lot of them these days."

Smiling, Cody recalled Jill's skepticism when he'd

tossed out the nickname for the Food and Drug Administration's Handbook on Pathogenic Microorganisms and Natural Toxins.

"Dr. Nez reported the virus," Long continued, all business now, "but indicated only limited incidence. A single isolated case, as I recall."

"We're up to four now and still counting."

"Have you reported them in system?"

"Not yet."

"Why?"

Cody hesitated. Even with Captain Westfall's concurrence and the knowledge that John had received special security briefings, he still had to dance around any mention of Pegasus.

"All the infected personnel were confined to a restricted area."

"No contact with communities or personnel outside that area?"

"Limited contact."

Cody, Jill and Bill Thompson had all made trips to Albuquerque. Then there was the run-in Jill and her MPs had with the two skinny-dippers up in the mountains.

Damn! With Bill's heart attack and the two subsequent cases piled right on top of the air evac, Cody had forgotten about that little incident. An unhappy rumble over the phone jerked his attention back to the head of the CDC.

"Not good," John was saying. "Not good at all.

It's imperative we make the surrounding communities aware of the appearance of a new strain of virus, along with its toxicology and potential for widespread infection.''

''I agree. That's why I contacted you. Before we input a sanitized version of the data, though, I want to make one more call.''

''Make it and get right back to me.''

''I will.''

It took Cody only a few minutes to get the names and phone numbers of the illicit lovers, another ten to track them both down. The sheriff's son-in-law grudgingly reported no fever, no dizziness, no achy joints either before or after his dip in the pool. His girlfriend, however, had been sick as a dog.

''I was so weak and dizzy my mother had to drive me to the E.R.,'' she informed Cody when he reached her at the county hospital. She'd been admitted less than twenty-four hours after her tryst in the mountains.

''The docs still don't know what hit me.''

''I do.''

''What?''

''It's a new strain of virus.''

''A virus?'' The woman's voice took on an edge of alarm. ''It's not, like, terminal is it?''

''It doesn't appear to be if the patient receives timely treatment, which you did. I've got the name of your admitting physician. I'll give him a call and advise him to run some tests just to be sure.''

Cody contacted the physician and told him to check the CDC database for the data Dr. Nez had input into the system. He also requested the doc report this case and additional ones to his local CDC officer immediately.

''I will, Dr…. What did you say your name was again?''

''Richardson. Cody Richardson. I'm with the Public Health Service,'' he repeated with deliberate vagueness.

He was back on the line with John Long within moments.

''We've got another patient. This one's a civilian. Her physician promised to advise CDC of her symptoms immediately. You can use her case as a means to spread the word to the surrounding communities.''

''That works.''

Cody hung up and blew out a long breath. They'd dodged that bullet. For a while, anyway, they could sit on the fact that four personnel from the Pegasus site had been infected with this vicious little bug.

He didn't find out a fifth troop had gone down until he searched out Captain Westfall.

He found the captain in the hangar. Like the proud owner of a Thoroughbred, the naval officer was gliding a hand along the smooth, sleek skin of the steed he hoped to race the following morning.

He glanced up at the sound of footsteps. His lean face relaxed into a rueful smile at being caught in a show of affection for a mere machine.

"The maintenance crews wired him up to the black boxes first thing this morning and checked every system," he said, giving the radar-evading composite fuselage a final pat. "He's all ready to run."

"Good."

"Assuming no more of our team comes down sick," the captain added, his penetrating gray eyes narrowed on Cody's face, "and you don't tell me we've all been tagged as disease carriers and confined to the site."

"Not yet. We may have our first reported case in the local community."

Briefly, he ran through his series of phone calls. Like Cody, the captain breathed a sigh of relief that they didn't have to go public with the events occurring at the Pegasus site.

Yet.

"This woman became infected within twenty-four hours of entering the restricted area," he warned.

"Which means she picked it up here."

"In all likelihood. But I still don't have a clue where or how. Apparently, she and her boyfriend drove separate cars to a rendezvous point a few miles from the White Sand spur, then went up into the mountains together.''

"Major Bradshaw responded to the scene and interviewed the couple, didn't she? Maybe she can shed some light on their movements.''

"Maybe.''

Sliding the flat, palm-size communicator out of his shirt pocket, Cody pressed the code for the chief of security. Jill didn't answer his page.

He tried again, holding the single key down until the small device beeped loudly, indicating the signal had gone through. Still no answer.

Frowning, he pressed the button for the MP Control Desk.

"Rattler Control.''

"This is Commander Richardson. I'm trying to contact Major Bradshaw but get no response.''

"Hold on, sir. She's still up in the mountains. The gullies and rock outcroppings may be blocking your signal. We'll raise her on our channel. We have a direct satellite link.''

Cody stared at the hangar's white-painted concrete floor until Rattler Control came back on.

"The major doesn't respond, sir.''

"When was the last time she checked in?''

"About forty minutes ago, according to the log. We require our patrols to check in once every hour, but the major usually doesn't go that long without someone needing to speak with her.'' A guarded note entered the controller's voice. "We'll keep trying to contact her, sir. In the meantime, I'll…"

He broke off, leaving Cody straining to hear the faint, static-filled transmission coming into the Control Center.

"Major Bradshaw's responding, sir! At least, I think she is."

"What do you mean, you think she is?"

"She didn't ID herself and her words are all slurred."

"Keep her on the line! I'll be right there." He snapped his device shut. "It's Jill. Something's wrong."

He was running for the hangar door before the words were out. Westfall pounded right behind him. Together they burst out of the hangar and raced across the compound to the modular unit housing Rattler Control.

A small contingent of MPs had gathered in the Control Center by the time Cody and the captain entered it. The soldiers edged aside to give them access, but hovered close to listen to the ensuing exchange.

"Rattler One, this is Rattler Control. I have Doc Richardson here with me. Do you read me, Rattler One?" The lanky Oklahoman gripped the mike. "Please acknowledge, Rattler One."

The response came in dazed and whisper soft. "Cody? You…there?"

He leaned forward, his chest tight. Jill wouldn't

break military protocol and call him by his first name with her troops listening in without damned good reason.

"I'm here. We're having trouble hearing you, Rattler One. Are you in distress?"

"Hot. I'm…hot."

"Are you saying you have a fever?"

"Burning up."

He glanced up, met Westfall's grim gaze. The Pegasus virus had struck again.

"And all…this damned…blood." The ragged whisper cut through the Control Center. "In my…eyes."

Cody's insides went ice-cold. "Why do you have blood in your eyes? Jill? Why is there blood in your eyes?"

"Fell. Hit my head. Rock. I'm so…tired, Cody. So sleepy."

"Jill! Listen to me. It sounds as though you might have sustained a concussion."

Compounded by the onset of a sudden high fever, the combination could be deadly. He fought the panic clawing at his gut and kept his tone calm.

"Describe your position. Are you lying down? Sitting up? Jill! Are you sitting up?"

"On…my…knees."

"That's good, sweetheart. That's good."

If she'd crawled onto her knees, she probably hadn't suffered spinal injury.

"What about your head laceration? Is it still bleeding?"

"Yes. No. I... I don't think so."

God, he hoped it wasn't. If she'd fractured her skull, he didn't want her applying pressure to the injured area in an attempt to stop the bleeding.

"Okay, I need you to sit down. Easy, Jill. Easy. Just roll onto your bottom and sit."

He held his breath until he heard a little grunt. When it tipped into a low moan, sweat pooled at the base of Cody's spine.

"Stay put now. Do *not* move." Lowering his voice, he drilled the controller. "We've got her location pinpointed, right?"

"That's affirmative, sir."

The controller jerked his chin at the console, which showed a digital map of the site. Jill was the blinking red dot in the far northeast corner of the map.

"You've got patrols out," Captain Westfall snapped. "How close is the nearest one?"

"Rattler Six is patrolling sector four, almost fifty miles to the southwest. Rattler Two is even farther, two hours or more from the major's position."

"What about the chopper?" Cody asked, whirling to face the captain. "Is it on-site?"

"No. With the test run delayed until tomorrow, the crew flew the bird up to Kirtland for some required maintenance."

"Hell!"

His chest tight, Cody fixed his eyes on that blinking red dot and forced a calm, steady transmission.

"I'll get to you as soon as I can, Jill. I'm leaving the site right now. Do you hear me? Jill! Do you hear me?"

"Yes."

It was a sigh, a whisper of sound that ripped the heart right out of his chest.

Alicia had died after sustaining massive head trauma. For a horrific moment Cody was once again standing in a sterile ICU, a consent form crushed in one fist, while machines pumped air into his wife's lungs.

He shook his head, shattering the image. This wasn't Alicia, the woman he'd loved and lost. This was Jill, and Cody was damned if he was going to lose her, too.

"I'm coming to you," he swore fiercely. "I'm coming. Just don't move."

He whirled and started for the door.

"I'll get my bag," he barked at the controller. "Have one of those souped-up Humvees ready to run."

"Yes, sir!"

Captain Westfall interceded. "We'll do better than a modified Humvee. You get your bag and I'll get hold of Major McIver."

"Mac? What do you want with…?" Cody stopped

dead. His eyes locked with those of the captain. ''Pegasus?''

''He's ready to run. Mac took him for his first gallop. He can take him out for this one, too. Go get your bag and meet us at the hangar.''

Chapter 15

By the time Cody raced back to the hangar with an emergency medical kit, Russ McIver had climbed into Pegasus's cockpit, fired up its engines, and rolled the vehicle out onto the tarmac where chocks were placed in front of its wheels.

It quivered like a finely bred racehorse ready to run. Sleek and gleaming white in the bright sun, Pegasus was in land mode. Its rotor blades were folded, the wings were swept back and tucked into the fuselage. The sturdy wheels that would carry it across gullies and up steep mountain slopes glistened clean and black.

Two modified Humvees bristling with armament stood ready to serve as chase vehicles. Captain Westfall was taking a chance sending a highly classified prototype vehicle out into the field without accompanying air cover. His tight jaw and the glint of steel in his gray eyes indicated he was more than willing to assume the risk.

"Bring her home, Doc."

"I will."

Cody tipped him a quick salute and ducked through the open side hatch. As soon as he was aboard, Mac closed the hatch. Cody strapped his medical kit into one of the side-facing passenger seats that ran the length of the fuselage and climbed into the cockpit. The buzz-cut marine in the operator's seat greeted him with a curt nod.

"Buckle up, Commander. You're in for one helluva ride."

He wasn't exaggerating.

Mac punched the coordinates of Jill's location into the on-board navigational system and did a final systems check. A quick thumbs-up to the ground crew sent them scuttling to remove the chocks.

Mac's right arm thrust the throttle forward. Like a lightning bolt hurled by an angry Zeus, Pegasus shot forward. The swift acceleration threw Cody back against his seat.

"Man, I can't wait to take this baby airborne," the marine muttered.

The airborne test phase would come next. For now Mac had to be content with sending the sleek, swept-wing vehicle shooting off the end of the concrete and onto the hard-packed sand. Not until he had the vehicle skimming across the desert on a direct vector to the mountains did his passenger draw in a full breath.

With air in his lungs again, Cody's first action was to request a satellite channel. Rattler Control patched him through on a direct link to Rattler One.

"Jill, it's Cody. Do you read me?"

His heart ticked off the seconds. One. Two. When ten or more had passed with no response, he tried again.

"Jill! Come in, please."

Still no answer. His fist cold and clammy on the mike, Cody shot the man next to him a grim look.

"Is this as fast as Pegasus can sprint?"

Mac tore his intent gaze from the instrument panel. "We're pushing the limit of the test parameters now."

"To hell with the test parameters. Open it up, Mac."

Captain Westfall was listening in with the others at Test Control. His deep, gravelly voice came over the intercom hard on the heels of Cody's terse demand.

"I'm authorizing a situational test deviation, Major. Take Pegasus to full land speed."

"Aye, aye, sir."

Mac flashed Cody a swift grin. His gloved fist wrapped around the throttle and shoved it forward. With a roar the engines kicked into overdrive.

A glance out the wraparound cockpit windows showed Pegasus churning up great spumes of sand from under its wide-track wheels. It also showed the chase vehicles falling well behind.

Within moments there was only the racing vehicle with its two occupants, the foothills looming dead ahead, and the continuing silence at the other end of the satellite link.

Jill kept hearing voices. Instructing her to do something. Not do something. She couldn't make out the exact words through the buzzing in her head.

Lord, it was hot! So burning, blistering hot! She was swimming in her own sweat.

Hot. Sweat. Fever.

A dim, shadowed scene formed in her mind. She saw a bed. A flushed soldier stretched out under a thin sheet. Cooling packs tucked around him.

The red mists in her head parted for a moment, only a moment. The fever spiking through her body could kill her. It *would* kill her if she didn't bring it down.

Panting, she tore at the buttons of her BDU shirt. She had to get it off. Had to douse the fire raging through her veins. Pain splintered through her skull as she dragged off the fire-retardant fabric. She tried to shed her heavy web belt with all its accoutrements, as well, but the buckle defeated her sweat-slick, fumbling fingers.

She felt a blessed relief for all of a moment or two, until the blazing sun heated her blood to boiling again, and small, biting gnats began to feast on the tender flesh left bare by her short-sleeved T-shirt.

The stinging bites were a mere annoyance at first, a vague distraction at the far edge of her mind. Seemingly in the next breath the swarm intensified, became a cloud that voraciously attacked the blood drying on the side of her face.

Jill stumbled to her feet. The world went black. She swayed, dizzy, disoriented, almost fell again. Sheer determination kept her upright.

A stream. She remembered crossing a stream. One that led to a rock basin and a pool. Cool. Shaded. Wet. Gritting her teeth, she swiped the sticky blood from her eyes with the back of her hand. Which way? Where was it?

Without knowing whether she was heading east or west, she staggered at a drunken angle across the slope. She left her shirt behind. The mangled remains of her ATV. Goofy. A sob rose in her throat as the image of a dog with a long muzzle and a silly grin slowly lengthened, thinned, began to writhe right in front of her eyes.

Snakes. She had to watch for snakes. Slithering. Hissing. Sinking their fangs into Sergeant Barnes, who suddenly materialized not ten yards away. He was beckoning to her, smiling at her, but with each stumbling step she took toward him, he, too, changed size and shape.

Cody! That was Cody with a smile crinkling the corners of his eyes. Cody urging her on. Cody who stood to gain millions if he sprayed something in Jill's nose.

Voices rang in her head again. One angry, filled with hate, spewing out an accusation of murder. Another deeper, rougher, husky with passion. Gradually, a muted roar was added to the voices, growing louder, drowning them out.

Gasping, her neck and arms slick with sweat, Jill swatted at the vicious little gnats and stumbled toward a stand of twisted piñon. Her boot caught on a squishy lump. She looked down, saw she'd buried her foot in the rotting carcass of another reptile.

The hot, bitter taste of bile rose in her throat.

Pegasus barely broke stride as he pawed his way up the steep, rocky slope. Mac leaned into his shoulder harness, his right hand working the joystick that guided the vehicle around trees and boulders.

Branches scraped the hull. The multiple-suspension tires absorbed shock after shock. Despite the rough ride, Cody kept his gaze locked on the navigational display indicating the remaining distance to the spot marked by a blinking red dot.

Two hundred meters.

One-fifty.

One hundred.

"That looks like an ATV. Or what's left of one."

Mac's grim pronouncement brought Cody's head whipping up.

"She must have jumped out of the ATV before it wrapped around that rock," he ground out. "The nav display is showing her another sixty plus meters farther up the slope."

Mac pushed Pegasus on. His heart pounding, Cody scanned the rocky terrain ahead for a glimpse of a black beret, honey-blond hair, blotchy-brown and tan fatigues, anything!

What he spotted was a splash of glistening red on an outcropping of jagged gray stone.

"Over there!"

Mac maneuvered Pegasus to a safe angle and hit the brakes. Cody was out of his seat and had his bag in hand before the hatch whirred open. Mac scrambled out after him scant seconds later. The crumpled, blood-soaked shirt lying beside the gray stone stopped both men in their tracks.

With a short, vicious curse, Cody dropped down on one knee, thrust a hand in the shirt pocket and pulled out a slim leather case. Inside was Jill's holographic ID with its embedded homing signal.

"She can't have gone far," he said grimly, pushing to his feet. "Not if she's concussed and burning with fever."

"Right," Mac concurred. "You angle down and to the right. I'll go up and to the left. We'll walk fifty meters, turn and work a grid."

The voices started again.

The roaring inside Jill's head had stopped, thank God, but now she heard someone—several some-ones—shouting in the distance. She was in the pool, the cool, shaded pool. She'd tucked her knees under her so the water could lap her chin and cheeks.

Even with a shroud of water wrapped around her up to her chin, fire still raged in her veins. Nauseous, dizzy, so confused she couldn't remember her name, she unfolded her legs. Some deep, hazy instinct had her struggling up. She was supposed to guard. Protect. Something…something important.

The weight of her bat belt almost dragged her back down into the pool. Finally she got her boots under her. Water sluiced down her body as she fumbled for the flap on her holster. Her hand wrapped around crosshatched steel.

The butt of the Beretta felt so familiar, so right. This was her job, her mission. To protect. To guard.

The scrabble of boots on rock brought her torso around and her arms up. She held the Beretta two-fisted, the way she'd been taught. The way she'd cradled it in countless sessions at the firing range. The way she'd steadied it before that last, murderous exchange of shots. Where? Kosevo? Baghdad?

A blurred figure crashed out of the trees to her left. Whirling, she squinted against the pain in her head and tried desperately to bring the shadowy figure into focus.

"Stop right there!"

She'd shouted the words. Why did they sound so low and hoarse, like the last croak of a dying frog.

Dying. They were all dying. The frogs. The snakes. The members of the test cadre.

"Jill."

The single word was deep. Quiet. Wary.

"Put the gun down."

"My job," she rasped. "My duty. Protect…at all costs."

She couldn't surrender her arms. She *wouldn't!* The figure took a step. Her finger locked on the trigger.

"Stay…there!" Had she pushed the safety to off?

She couldn't remember. Oh, God, she couldn't remember!

"It's Cody, Jill. I told you I'd come for you. I'm here, sweetheart. I'm here."

The slow, deep resonance penetrated the pain pinwheeling through her skull.

"Put the gun down, Jill. It's me. Cody."

She knew him. Knew the name. How? Why? The answer burst in her head like a Roman candle.

Cody Richardson killed her.

My baby.

He killed her.

Dead snakes. Dead babies. The images brought bile back up into her throat. Her knuckles whitened. Her finger squeezed against the trigger.

The figure moved closer, waded into the pool.

"Stop!"

He ignored her. Took another. Two. Until she couldn't possibly miss.

She locked her knees, sighted on the spot squarely between his eyes. His calm, steady blue eyes.

She knew those eyes. They'd smiled down at her. Just before he kissed her.

"Let me help you," he said slowly, quietly, and reached for her weapon.

A sharp crack split the air.

Russ McIver had spent enough years in uniform

to recognize the report of a pistol when he heard it. His first instinct was to drop into a crouch. His second had him reaching for his radio.

"Doc! This is Mac. Did you just fire a signal shot?"

He waited, his jaw clenched.

"Doc, this is Mac. Come in please."

When the radio remained silent, the marine cursed viciously and charged back down the slope.

Chapter 16

Cody was on his knees at the edge of the pool when Russ McIver came pounding up.

The marine skidded to a halt. His glance zinged from the rivulets of blood running down Cody's arm to the woman stretched out on the ground beside him.

"What happened?"

"Jill's gun went off."

"She *shot* you?"

"Not intentionally."

Cody was almost sure of that. He'd reached for the Beretta at the same instant her legs had collapsed under her. The combination of her sagging weight and his tentative grip on the barrel had sent a bullet right through the sleeve of his khaki uniform. It missed the bone, thank God, but had taken out a chunk of his skin and muscle.

The flesh wound didn't worry him. Jill did. His initial exam indicated a lacerated scalp and probable concussion. He wouldn't know for sure whether she'd fractured her skull until he got her into X-ray.

She'd also suffered severe dehydration from the heat and the fever raging through her body. Her confusion and near delirium could be ascribed to the blow to her head, but her decreased tissue turgor, mottled limbs and rapid, thready pulse had told him she needed an infusion of fluid and fast.

Gritting his teeth against the pain in his arm, Cody ripped the plastic off the packet of IV solution he'd extracted from his bag, spiked the port and squeezed the life-saving liquid into the drip chamber.

"Hold the bag."

The terse order brought Mac jumping forward. He positioned the packet waist-high while Cody inserted a length of coiled plastic tubing and squeezed fluid through it to expel the air bubbles. Once the solution ran freely, a twist of the flow clamp stopped it.

The bite of a rubber tourniquet six inches above her elbow drew Jill's brows together. Frowning, she lifted her lids. "What…? What are you doing?"

The glazed look in her eyes hurt him worse than his wound.

"It's okay, sweetheart. I'm just starting an IV."

He worked swiftly, cleansing the insertion site

with a Betadine wipe, sliding in the needle, yanking the rubber tourniquet free.

Only after he'd adjusted the clamp and started the flow did he lift an arm to swipe at the sweat beading his forehead. Too late he realized it was the same arm Jill had put a bullet through. Swearing, he ground his jaws together against the burning ache.

"We need to give the IV a few minutes to infiltrate before we transport her back to base," he told Mac. "In the meantime, it would help to wet her down again."

"I'm on it, Doc. Hold the bag."

Dragging off his helmet, the marine tossed it aside and waded into the pool. He didn't give a thought to the electronics built into the sophisticated headgear, nor did Cody. One of their own was down.

The combination of the IV and a cool, soothing soak worked miracles. Within a remarkably short period of time, Jill had recovered enough to mumble out the right answer when asked her name. Only then did Cody push up his sleeve and tend to his still-sluggishly bleeding wound.

When he deemed Jill stable enough to move, however, she seemed to sink back into delirium.

"Snakes," she muttered as he eased her into a sitting position.

"What?"

"I saw snakes." She gave her head a confused little shake. "Stepped on one."

Cody's stomach dropped clear to his boots. ''Were you bitten? Jill! Answer me! Were you bitten?''

''Don't...think so.''

Hell! He'd been treating her for the blow to her head and raging fever. It hadn't even occurred to him she might have sustained another injury. Ignoring the scream of protest from his injured arm, he tore at the laces of Jill's boots and yanked them off.

''Cody, I...''

''Stay still!''

He disposed of her socks and soggy pants next. He groaned when he saw the fire-engine-red bikini panties she wore under her uniform, and almost wept with relief when he found no irritated swelling or fang marks on her feet, ankles or legs.

''Come on,'' he growled, ''let's get you out of here. Mac, hold that IV bag high.''

''The snakes...''

''They're gone, Jill. It's just you, me and Mac.''

''No!''

Agitated, she grabbed his injured arm. The yank had him gritting his teeth.

''They were dead, Cody. The snakes. They were dead.''

''It's okay, babe. You're just a little confused.''

''I'm not hallucinating, dammit!'' Her brow furrowed. ''Or am I? No, I saw them. They were dead.''

Wincing, he tried to ease his arm out of her tight grip. ''Okay, they were dead.''

Her fingers dug into him, refusing to let go. "Like our mascot, Cody. They were dead and they had gnats swarming all around them. *Just like Sergeant Barnes's rattler.*"

That got his attention. He dropped back on his heels, staring at her while his mind worked furiously.

Was that it? Had Jill stumbled on the answer? Were the snakes in this area the source of the new, mutant virus? Was it being transmitted by the stinging little gnats everyone swatted at but no one paid much attention to?

The insects were a minor annoyance down at the compound, where the dry desert air kept them at bay. Up here in the mountains, they swarmed thicker and darker and bred in...

In pools like this one!

Excitement shot through his veins. The researcher in him wanted a sample and immediate access to a lab. The physician had only one concern. His patient.

Only after he'd scooped her up, his teeth grinding at the pain in his arm, did he realize the researcher and the physician had both taken a back seat to the man. He was just now beginning to recover from that fear that had tied him in knots.

He could have lost her. Might still lose her if he didn't get her back to the clinic and control the fever still heating her skin.

As he pushed to his feet, a protesting Mac stepped forward. "You're hit, doc. I'll carry her."

"I've got her. You manage the IV."

Cody would always swear the subsequent twenty-four hours shaved a good ten years off his life.

Pegasus got them down to the desert and streaked back to the compound. Mac radioed in a condensed version of the events on the mountain. Captain Westfall wasn't the kind of man given to cheers, but when Mac advised that they'd found Major Bradshaw and were returning her to base, the whoops and shouts of the others at Test Control echoed through the headphones.

Two of Cody's hospital corpsmen were waiting at the hangar. They bundled Jill onto a stretcher and rushed her to the clinic. Cody delayed only long enough to brief Captain Westfall on the possible source of the virus.

"Get Sergeant Barnes to exhume the remains of his pet. We need to send them up to Decker Labs."

"I'll take care of it," the captain promised. "You take care of Jill."

"Yes, sir."

The promise was easier than the doing.

Her head laceration was just that, a deep laceration. X-rays showed no fracture and the cut itself required only a couple of stitches. The possibility of a concussion combined with her high fever continued to worry him. Despite cooling packs and a continuous IV drip, her temperature spiked off and on for the rest of that day.

Luckily Cody's other two patients had made a full recovery. He discharged Private Harris late that afternoon. The cook went back to his quarters early that evening. Only Jill remained at the clinic, flushed, feverish, fretful.

Cody stayed with her all through the night. When her fever spiked again around three in the morning, he came close, very close, to ordering a medical evacuation to Albuquerque. The hospital couldn't do anything for her he wasn't already doing, but his gut took another twist with every degree her temperature shot up.

Finally, it leveled off at 102 and she dropped into an exhausted slumber. Cody sprawled in the chair beside her bed and kept from sliding into sleep himself by listing all the reasons he'd come to love this woman.

She was smart. Stubborn. Tough. Vulnerable. Sexy as hell in *and* out of those red bikini briefs. The first time they'd met, she'd had him facedown in the dirt. The wild, soul-searing hours they'd spent together in Albuquerque had rocked him right back on his heels. Today…

Yesterday, he amended silently, scraping a palm over the stubble on his chin. Yesterday the woman had put a bullet through him. A wry smile tipped his mouth as he wondered what else she'd put him through in the next twenty or thirty years. Major Jill Bradshaw didn't know it yet, but Cody fully intended to become her full-time, attending physician.

Jill woke to a dry, gritty throat that felt as though it had gobbled down half the desert. Dragging up sandpapery lids, she focused her blurry gaze on the figure leaning over her. As he stuck something in her ear, she decided he looked as grungy as she felt.

The bristly beginnings of a beard shadowed his cheeks and chin. Weariness had etched deep grooves on either side of his mouth. When he bent over her, his white lab coat gaped open to show a rumpled khaki uniform streaked with dirt and brown, splotchy stains.

"Cody?"

He glanced down at her, a smile in his blue eyes.

"Hi. Hold still a moment."

He removed the object from her ear. It was a thermometer, Jill saw, and whatever the little device recorded must have pleased him. His mouth relaxed into a smile that matched the one in his eyes.

"How do you feel?"

"Like someone ran over me with a Humvee."

"That good, huh? Want to suck on some ice chips?"

"Yes!"

"Hang loose, I'll get you some."

Since she was hooked up to an IV and as weak as a baby, Jill didn't see she had a whole lot of choice.

It wasn't Cody who delivered the ice chips a few moments later, however, but her two roommates.

"Hey, girl!" Kate exclaimed. "The doc said you were awake and lucid this time."

"This time?"

"You've been pretty well out of it since he brought you down from the mountain yesterday morning."

Cari dug a spoon into a plastic container and held it out. "Here you go."

Jill sucked on the ice chips greedily, swallowed and begged for more.

"We'd better sit you up," Kate said, searching for the mechanism to raise the back of the bed. She hit the button, eased the patient up and untangled the sheet. Her green eyes glinted as she drew it over Jill's lower half.

"Those are some eye-popping panties, by the way. Every male at the scene did a double take when Cody carried you out of Pegasus."

"What are you talking about?"

"He didn't tell you?"

"Tell me what?"

"The story he gave us," Kate drawled, "is that he stripped you down to search for a possible snake-bite."

Jill gulped down the icy chips. A snake. She remembered a snake. A black-tail. Dead.

"Of course," the irrepressible weather officer added with a grin, "the strip act came after you pumped a bullet into him. One has to wonder if the doc was just getting some of his own back."

Jill choked on the ice.

"I shot him?"

"You did."

She remembered drawing her weapon now. She even remembered why. Vaguely.

There was a call. From Jack Conway. He accused Cody of killing his daughter.

Then there was that business with the virus and the fact that it had only infected people at the Pegasus site. That had preyed on Jill's mind all during the drive up to the higher elevations until…

Until Cody had appeared out of nowhere, walked into her pistol sight, and everything blurred again.

"Well," she muttered, her throat raw and tight, "that explains the splotchy red stains on his uniform."

"He wouldn't leave you long enough to change into a clean one," Cari told her gently. "Even when that lab in Albuquerque wanted him to fly up and verify their findings."

"Decker Labs? What did they find?"

"Exactly what you suggested they would," Cody answered, strolling back into the ward. "A very rare, very isolated disease that apparently infects only the large-fanged snakes in this particular corner of New Mexico.''

"Right," Kate quipped. "Large-fanged snakes. As opposed to…?"

"Rear-fanged and small-fanged," he replied, grinning.

"I think I just exceeded my limit on what I want to know about fangs of any kind," Cari said with a delicate shudder. "Come on, Kate, let's leave the doc to tend to his patient."

The flame-haired weather officer gave Jill's shoulder a pat. "Get back on your feet quick, sweetie. Now that Cody's pinned down the source of our mysterious bug and Pegasus passed his mountain run with flying colors, Captain Westfall is ready to move us into Phase II."

"Bill Thompson's replacement is supposed to arrive on-site in the next couple of days," Cari explained, yielding the plastic pitcher of ice to Cody. "As soon as he's in place and you're on your feet, we're back in business."

The curtain dropped behind the two women, leaving Jill to demand the details from Cody.

"What's the source of our bug, and when did Pegasus pass his mountain run?"

"The answer to the first question is gnats," he told her as he reclaimed his seat beside her bed. "The answer to the second is yesterday. Open up."

Jill accepted a spoon full of ice chips and listened while he calmly explained that the dead snakes she'd stumbled across had been infected with a hitherto unknown variant of a virus transmitted by tiny, stinging little gnats. In the past twenty-four hours, searchers had found more than a dozen more dead reptiles.

"The Center for Disease Control is speculating that this disease has similar characteristics to EHD— Epizootic hemorrhagic disease. It affects white-tailed deer and pronghorn antelope only in the driest months, when they congregate at waterholes where gnats breed. The difference is EHD is rarely transmitted to humans."

"Well, thank God that mystery's solved."

Jill decided she really didn't need to tell Cody she'd entertained the hazy notion that he or Jack Conway might have deliberately introduced the bug into the Pegasus site. She was a cop. It was her business to suspect everyone, even the man she was pretty sure she'd tumbled into love with.

She knew for certain just moments later, when he pulled a small plastic toy out of the pocket of his lab coat.

"Where did you find him?"

"Right where you left him. Your troops had to take what remained of your ATV apart to get the pieces back to the site. I asked them to retrieve Goofy. I thought you might like to have him looking over your shoulder while you recover your strength."

Since the outbreak of sickness at the site, Cody probably hadn't snatched more than a few hours of sleep. He'd been tending to patients, trying to figure out the source of their infection, and attempting to identify a rare variation of a bug. He'd just taken a bullet in the arm. According to Kate, he'd carried Jill to Pegasus, then hauled her out again. Despite everything else coming down on him, he'd still remembered her old buddy.

Jill never cried. Not since she'd strapped on a sidearm, anyway. Yet she couldn't quite swallow the silly, sloppy sniffle that accompanied her gruff request.

"Stick him in the drawer, Doc."

He cocked a brow. "You sure? I thought he was your good luck charm."

"I'm sure. You're the only one I want looking over my shoulder while I recover."

Or anytime else.

She didn't say it. She didn't have to. He said it for her.

"I'll take good care of you," he promised softly. "Real good."

He kept his promise.

Jill's fever had subsided completely by the following morning. By midafternoon, she was bathed, dressed in a clean hospital gown, up and prowling the ward. Her head throbbed dully with the aftereffects of a mild concussion, but she was antsy and impatient to get back to work.

Cody refused to release her. She discovered why later that evening, when he strolled into the ward area.

"Helluva a thing when two adults have to sneak around to neck," he commented.

She slanted him a startled look. "Are we going to neck?"

"Oh, yeah."

"What about Specialist Ingalls?"

"I sent her to the chow hall for supper."

"She might eat fast."

"I locked the clinic door."

The wicked gleam in his eyes stopped her breath.

"Ever wonder why hospital gowns open down the back?" he asked, reaching behind her for the tie that held hers at the neck.

"Not anymore," she replied with a shaky chuckle.

Her laughter ended on a strangled gulp when he dipped his head and dropped a tender kiss on her scar. The gulp gave way to a sensual groan as his lips trailed along her bare shoulder.

"Any chance this session is going to go further than necking?" she asked with a catch in her voice.

"Nope." He nuzzled the hollow just above her collarbone. "I'm too weak for anything more. You shot me, remember?"

If he was weak, she was Cleopatra, Queen of the

Nile. But Jill had to admit there was something exquisitely pleasurable in his gentle, roving hands and the warm wash of his breath against her skin.

Not to mention his husky admission when he raised his head and caught her gaze.

"I think you should know I'm considering appointing myself your personal physician for the next twenty or thirty years."

"You are, huh?" Her hand came up to cup his cheek. "How about we see Pegasus through his final paces, then talk about it?"

"How about we talk about it now, and get married after we see Pegasus through his final paces? Or engaged," he amended at her startled gasp. "I don't want to push you."

"I can see that!"

His expression sobered, and a trace of the regret Jill had glimpsed when he'd told her about his wife came into his eyes.

"I realized something up there on the mountain. Listening to you struggle for every breath when your fever spiked only reinforced it. I love you, Jill. I don't want to look back five or ten or twenty years from now and kick myself for not telling you when I had the chance. I intend to keep telling you until you get tired of hearing it."

She had to fight for breath again, only this time it wasn't due to a fever. "Sounds…sounds like a plan to me."

"Good! We're engaged to get engaged."

His crooked grin melted the last of Jill's resistance. That and the long, heart-hammering kiss he gave her.

Matching his grin, she nodded. "We're engaged to be engaged."

*   *   *   *   *

Be sure to watch for the next book in
TO PROTECT AND DEFEND,
*coming from Silhouette Desire
in January 2004, when sparks fly
in FULL THROTTLE.*

Coming in December 2003
to Silhouette Books

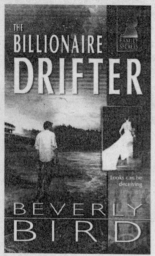

THE
BILLIONAIRE
DRIFTER

by

BEVERLY
BIRD

Disguised as a beach bum, billionaire Max Strong
wants to hide from the glitz and glamour of his
life—until he meets a beautiful stranger who
seduces him and then mysteriously disappears....

**Look for more titles in this exhilarating new series,
available only from Silhouette Books.**

Five extraordinary siblings.
One dangerous past.
Unlimited potential.

✂

Your opinion is important to us! Please take a few moments to share your thoughts with us about your experiences with Harlequin and Silhouette books. Your comments will be very useful in ensuring that we deliver books you love to read. *Please take a few minutes to complete the questionnaire, then send it to us at the address below.*

Send your completed questionnaires to:
Harlequin/Silhouette Reader Survey, P.O. Box 9046, Buffalo, NY 14269-9046

---

1. As you may know, there are many different lines under the Harlequin and Silhouette brands. Each of the lines is listed below. Please check the box that most represents your reading habit for each line.

Line	Currently read this line	Do not read this line	Not sure if I read this line
Harlequin American Romance	❑	❑	❑
Harlequin Duets	❑	❑	❑
Harlequin Romance	❑	❑	❑
Harlequin Historicals	❑	❑	❑
Harlequin Superromance	❑	❑	❑
Harlequin Intrigue	❑	❑	❑
Harlequin Presents	❑	❑	❑
Harlequin Temptation	❑	❑	❑
Harlequin Blaze	❑	❑	❑
Silhouette Special Edition	❑	❑	❑
Silhouette Romance	❑	❑	❑
Silhouette Intimate Moments	❑	❑	❑
Silhouette Desire	❑	❑	❑

2. Which of the following best describes why you bought *this book?* One answer only, please.

the picture on the cover	❑	the title	❑
the author	❑	the line is one I read often	❑
part of a miniseries	❑	saw an ad in another book	❑
saw an ad in a magazine/newsletter	❑	a friend told me about it	❑
I borrowed/was given this book	❑	other: _____	❑

3. Where did you buy *this book?* One answer only, please.

at Barnes & Noble	❑	at a grocery store	❑
at Waldenbooks	❑	at a drugstore	❑
at Borders	❑	on eHarlequin.com Web site	❑
at another bookstore	❑	from another Web site	❑
at Wal-Mart	❑	Harlequin/Silhouette Reader	❑
at Target	❑	Service/through the mail	
at Kmart	❑	used books from anywhere	❑
at another department store or mass merchandiser	❑	I borrowed/was given this book	❑

4. On average, how many Harlequin and Silhouette books do you buy at one time?

I buy _____ books at one time	❑
I rarely buy a book	❑

MRQ403SIM-1A

5. How many times per month do you shop for any *Harlequin and/or Silhouette* books?
One answer only, please.

1 or more times a week	❑	a few times per year	❑
1 to 3 times per month	❑	less often than once a year	❑
1 to 2 times every 3 months	❑	never	❑

6. When you think of your ideal heroine, which *one* statement describes her the best?
One answer only, please.

She's a woman who is strong-willed	❑	She's a desirable woman	❑
She's a woman who is needed by others	❑	She's a powerful woman	❑
She's a woman who is taken care of	❑	She's a passionate woman	❑
She's an adventurous woman	❑	She's a sensitive woman	❑

7. The following statements describe types or genres of books that you may be
interested in reading. Pick *up to 2 types* of books that you are most interested in.

I like to read about truly romantic relationships	❑
I like to read stories that are sexy romances	❑
I like to read romantic comedies	❑
I like to read a romantic mystery/suspense	❑
I like to read about romantic adventures	❑
I like to read romance stories that involve family	❑
I like to read about a romance in times or places that I have never seen	❑
Other: _____	❑

*The following questions help us to group your answers with those readers who are
similar to you. Your answers will remain confidential.*

8. Please record your year of birth below.
19 ____

9. What is your marital status?

single ❑   married ❑   common-law ❑   widowed ❑
divorced/separated ❑

10. Do you have children 18 years of age or younger currently living at home?
yes ❑   no ❑

11. Which of the following best describes your employment status?

employed full-time or part-time ❑   homemaker ❑   student ❑
retired ❑   unemployed ❑

12. Do you have access to the Internet from either home or work?
yes ❑   no ❑

13. Have you ever visited eHarlequin.com?
yes ❑   no ❑

14. What state do you live in?
_____

15. Are you a member of Harlequin/Silhouette Reader Service?
yes ❑   Account # _____   no ❑   MRQ403SIM-1B

Silhouette®

INTIMATE MOMENTS™

A new miniseries by popular author

RaeAnne Thayne

THE SEARCHERS

Finding family
where they least expected it...

Beginning with

Nowhere To Hide
(Silhouette Intimate Moments #1264)

Single mother Lisa Connors was trying to
protect her little girls. But when she met her
new next-door neighbor, handsome FBI agent
Gage McKinnon, she knew her heart was
in danger, as well....

**And coming soon from Silhouette Intimate
Moments—the rest of the McKinnons' stories.**

*Available December 2003
at your favorite retail outlet.*

COMING NEXT MONTH

SIMCNM1103